*A PETER O*  *:K*

Mercury

By the same author

A Charmed Circle
Let Me Alone
Asylum Piece (*stories*)
Change the Name
I Am Lazarus (*stories*)
Sleep Has His House
A Scarcity of Love
Eagles' Nest
A Bright Green Field
Who Are You?
Ice
Julia and the Bazooka (*stories*)
My Soul in China (*novella and stories*)

Anna Kavan

Mercury

With a Foreword by
Doris Lessing

Peter Owen
London & Chester Springs PA

PETER OWEN PUBLISHERS
73 Kenway Road London SW5 ORE
Peter Owen books are distributed in the USA by
Dufour Editions Inc. Chester Springs PA 19425-0007

First published in Great Britain 1994
© The Estate of Anna Kavan 1994

All Rights Reserved.
No part of this publication may be reproduced in
any form or by any means without the written
permission of the publishers.

ISBN 0-7206-0940-2

A catalogue record for this book is available from
the British Library

Printed and made in Great Britain by
Biddles of Guildford and King's Lynn

Foreword

This glittering hallucinogenic novel is surely one of the best of the books inspired by drug-taking. Not that you think, while you read, that this is drug-induced fantasy, rather that you have entered a realm of the marvellous, like a latter-day Ancient Mariner compelled to follow the tale, hypnotized by this story-teller who is at last getting the attention she deserves. The first chapter is as wonderful as any I remember, like the song of the lemurs it describes, who sing at sunrise and at sunset hidden among the leaves of the forest canopy, a gentle population both real and fantastical, like all the rest of the people and events in the story.

Doris Lessing

The words of Mercury are harsh after the songs of Apollo,

Love's Labour's Lost, V.ii

Mercury

1

THE densely massed foliage of the jungle swells like a sea of huge black cushions against the last phase of the night sky, where a faint transparency is already perceptible in the east. One after another the big bright stars are losing their brilliance; they fade and go out one by one.

The nebulous lightening of the east extends and intensifies, opening out into a great rose-gold fan, its incandescent sticks being the advance rays the rising sun shoots ahead over the horizon – blazing upward streams which produce an effect not unlike that of the aurora borealis, except that they substitute heat and colour for icy dazzle.

Life is just beginning to stir in the depths of the dim leafy ocean below. When suddenly, from the deepest and darkest thickets of this tropical forest unexplored by man, comes an extraordinary musical chiming, as of innumerable crystal bells; an amazing sound, utterly unexpected in that place, melodious and of limpid purity, which is only the prelude to the still more astounding chorus that follows. All at once, many voices, none of them human, burst into song together, rising and falling in eerie harmony; their sound doesn't belong to this world at all. At the same time the sun leaps into the sky, gilding the sides of tree-trunks and branches and lighting gold flames on myriads of leaves.

Only somebody up in the sky would be able to watch the stir that begins now in the topmost branches of certain trees, which seem to be blowing about in a strong wind, restricted to these trees alone, as the mysterious singers start moving, singing as they go, towards another outburst of similar singing not far away. From the ground it's quite impossible to see them leaping lightly from tree to tree; they are the whole time completely hidden by the dense foliage, the violent swaying of which, only visible from above, affords a clue to their size, as well as tracing their rapid progress.

The legend of the dog-headed man is said to have originated in these rare man-sized lemurs which are called Indris, now almost extinct, found nowhere but in the forests of this one remote tropical island. With perfect balance and muscular control they fly through the air like birds in great effortless bounds, all their movements soundless in spite of their size, and as sure and accurate in the dangerous tree-tops as a human being's on solid ground. When the two choirs meet there is no need of adjustment, they simply continue singing together in perfect unison, so that the surrounding forest rings with their combined voices.

Even the youngest of them join in, though they, out of sheer high spirits, have been indulging in all sorts of pranks and acrobatics as they travelled along, using the lianas as airy swings and walking precarious tightropes on the slenderest, loftiest boughs, but never letting these gymnastics delay the others.

The song has a distinct, regular rhythm, sinking to a gentle croon between the mounting waves of the central refrain; which is consistently repeated throughout, always clearly distinguishable, although with numerous variations and elaborations of the main theme, the singers showing great virtuosity in this proliferation of musical sounds. The uncanny strangeness of the singing, totally unlike man-made music, has its own fascination. But the most extraordinary thing of all is the way the song – in spite of its wordlessness and its inhuman quality – seems closely related to all forms of life on this planet, towards which it expresses an attitude entirely different from ours, as if giving a glimpse of another, quite different life, which could be lived here on earth – possibly even *is* being lived already somewhere in secret.... Attempting to translate into human terms, one can only say the singing is the symbol of aspiration ... of that deeply felt longing for something or somewhere else ... with which we react instinctively to the violence and cruelty endemic in our existence.

The concert ends as suddenly as it began. Not once during the performance have the Indris been visible from the ground; and they are no more visible now, screened by the many leaves of the tallest and largest trees, where they recline at ease or play in the branches, with many affectionate interludes, innocent caresses and kisses exchanged in a spontaneous overflowing of their general happiness and goodwill. The goodwill extends to their whole environment: in feeding each other with flower petals they detach the blooms with the utmost delicacy – not a leaf is accidentally damaged, not a twig broken or bent. Now that their singing is over, they are as silent as they are unseen, so noiseless in all their movements that a human watcher could actually be under the tree where their varied activities were taking place, and still remain unaware that the lemurs were anywhere near.

They have no enemies in their jungle world. And one naturally shrinks from naming that ferocious enemy who must have taught them their protective invisibility, so that they pass their whole lives unseen, never leaving the inmost secrecy of the forest. Their happy harmless community seems content with this hidden existence, spending the hours among the crowding massed leaves in peace, playfulness and affection, until the setting sun gives the signal for their second concert: which starts off with the same suddenness, and incorporates many of the same harmonies as the first, but is by no means a mere repetition of the dawn chorus. Indeed, as it continues, so many modifications are introduced that the result is a quite different complex of musical sounds, and conveys a quite different feeling... subdued, even melancholy....

Constantly falling cadences keep suggesting the end of something. The plaintive melody builds up a sense of loss, of finality, of nothing more being left, which is profoundly sad.

Yet, in the midst of the mournful passages, again and again there's a reprise, the original refrain reappearing as an assurance that there's been no break in continuity, a reaffirmation of the singers' former declaration of otherness... other values... introducing a hopeful note at the very point where a tragic climax might seem imminent and inevitable.

But then, immediately afterwards, sombre low notes restore the later version, so that two different conclusions are presented simultaneously and without any perceptible bias towards either.... In the end one is left to choose between them; a choice implying the non-existence of a fixed or final form of reality, for which is substituted the idea of all eventualities being equally plausible or unlikely.

2

THE man who'd brought the car round from the hotel garage stood beside it, waiting rather unhopefully for his tip. As the owner came down the steps he looked as if tips were far from his thoughts, wearing the aloof, somewhat forbidding expression that was habitual to him, although it was not in fact natural, but had been assumed years before to conceal the secret of his isolation. He always felt this as a lack in himself, as if some quality essential to human beings had been omitted in his case, so that he was perpetually at a disadvantage, and incapable of contact with them. Words and gestures that came naturally to everyone else, he could reproduce only by a deliberate effort, having failed to acquire even the small change of conversation. He frowned now when the other man saluted and asked politely how far he was going; but was compelled by his social uneasiness and the desire to hide it to answer briefly: 'Just to see some friends in the country.'

'Weather forecast's not too good, sir. They say we're in for a real freeze-up.'

Making a non-committal sound, Luke felt in his pocket and handed over a substantial tip, which enabled him to drive off without any more talk. The fear, involved even in exchanging the barest commonplaces, of betraying his secret and thus incurring hostility or suspicion, increased the vicious circle of his isolation. However, he was resigned to it on the whole (only at rare unnerving moments feeling as though he weren't real and would finally be consigned to oblivion without having lived at all), and spent most of his time in tremendous travels in remote parts of the world. Now, having just returned from a long stay in the tropics, the thought of freeze-ups was almost welcome to him.

*

It seemed much colder in the country, and, after driving for a long time, he found his thoughts turning nostalgically to a certain tropical forest and its inhabitants – weird singing creatures that had caught his imagination – but was forced to concentrate on the car. Darkness had already fallen and he knew he was lost – he should have arrived hours ago. Apart from occasional glints struck by the headlights from crusts of ice in the ruts of the narrow lane, there wasn't a gleam of light anywhere. He might have been driving through uninhabited country. Cold, anxious, depressed, he suddenly felt more alone and lost than he ever had in his adventurous travels; and exasperatingly helpless, trapped by the meanderings of the deserted lane, longing for a signpost to point the way to a main road.

Gradually he was beginning to wish he'd never embarked on this expedition. Of course he'd wanted to see Luz and her husband before doing anything else, as they were his only close friends. But he should have rung up beforehand to ask the way, instead of deciding to pay them a surprise visit. He wouldn't admit to any doubt as to the warmth of his reception. Nevertheless, his carefully fostered but not very real confidence had been shaken by the man at the garage where he'd stopped to fill up with petrol, whose words seemed to have cast an inauspicious blight over the entire project.

*

The friendly, cheerful young man, looking more like a farm-hand than a mechanic, hovers round the car, full of admiration for this new model, the first he has seen; and Luke, feeling obliged to return the compliment by saying something, asks if he knows how far it is to the village he's making for and whether he knows it.

Oh yes, he knows it all right. He's even been there in the summer – he thinks it's another ten miles or so. He still sounds as friendly as ever, but somehow contrives to convey that no one but a lunatic would go to such an out-of-the-way spot at this time of year, adding that he'll never find it unless he gets there in daylight. Since there's no chance of this as dusk is falling already, the last remark seems meant to arouse apprehension, in spite of its cheery tone.

Wanting to get away from the man at once, Luke cuts short the directions he's giving and drives off, ignoring his shout, which must be intended as a warning that he's in a one-way street, for a policeman stops him next moment and sends him back. All the same, he doesn't want to pass the garage again, and to avoid it, turns down a narrow alley which leads to a perfect maze of back streets, from which, owing to the complex system of traffic control, he has some difficulty in extricating himself, wasting ten minutes or more in the process; so that by the time he finally reaches open country it has got quite dark.

*

Although he told himself he didn't attach any significance to the fellow's remarks, he wished they hadn't been made; wishing still more that he hadn't interrupted his complicated directions – not that he could see to follow them. The headlights revealed only wayside vegetation and an occasional cottage or barn. There seemed to be a few more buildings here: but, as they flashed past, they all had the same dark, deserted look, and, as far as he could see, were all equally dilapidated. His nameless uneasiness grew stronger, associated now with these neglected dwellings and with the leafless unpruned hedges towering like secretive walls on both sides of the road. A vivid memory, retained from his last visit, of lush smiling summer country, absolutely refused to be reconciled with his present impression of general decay. It was possible, though extremely unlikely, that the road avoided all the villages . . . but why should the scattered buildings he passed all be unlit and apparently in varying stages of disintegration, as if they'd been abandoned and left to fall down? It almost looked as if a wholesale catastrophe had devastated the district while he'd been away. . . .

His discomfort intensified as he gradually got tired and hungry. His eyes started to ache from the close watch he had to keep all the time on the frozen road. He'd quite forgotten the strain of hours of night driving on rough icy slippery country lanes, which made the garage man's words seem less unreasonable. He'd never been very robust physically, and the wandering exile's life he had chosen in the hope of escaping from his own shortcomings had to some extent undermined his constitution. A few years back a severe attack of jaundice had been complicated by a tropical fever, and he still hadn't entirely got over the after-effects of this serious illness, which had been followed by a protracted enforced convalescence at a hotel in the south. It was here that he had first met Luz, who later married his friend Chas.

*

It's winter and there's hardly anyone staying in the place. On the evening of his arrival he looks gloomily round the almost empty dining-room, anticipating a future of dismal boredom, and half wishing himself back at the clinic he has just left.

Next moment, he gets a shock, startled suddenly by the extraordinary hair of a girl sitting near him – loose, flowing, shoulder-length, it is silvery-white, like an albino's. Her whole appearance is slightly odd, even without that bright floss of hair. She is extremely pale and excessively thin – he feels he can almost see through her, almost as if she were made of Venetian glass. There seems to be some pathos in her heart-shaped face, which has a look of timid, childlike submissiveness and big bright eyes the indefinable colour of clean stones under very clear water. He never notices girls as a rule; but he can't stop looking at this one, experiencing each time the same queer little shock, which seems to be half a shudder and half a thrill.

His long illness has left him physically weak and depleted, and in a rather peculiar mental state. He has a curious sense of having been through some form of punishment, or purification, which he connects with the attraction this fragile glass girl immediately has for him, with her delicate bones, silvery spun-glass hair, and pale, flawless, almost transparent skin. The very next day he gets to know her mother, who, bored in the out-of-season hotel, wants someone to talk to, and is glad of his company.

His progress with the daughter is much slower. She's always withdrawn and quiet, seems listless and lacking in energy, as if she too were recovering from an illness – far from discouraging him, he regards this as a sign of a mysterious bond between them. Each day he's more fascinated, drawn to her irresistibly, at first without realizing that his feeling is based on something slightly perverse. As soon as it strikes him that everything about her – her docile obedience to her mother, the resigned poses her frail graceful body assumes, her inordinately large anxious eyes – suggests a predestined victim, he makes up his mind to marry her, so that he'll be in a position to protect her from the brutality of the world, which her fragile, vulnerable aspect seems to invite.

He is considerably amazed by his own decision, for intimacy has never seemed possible for him. A nameless barrier always prevents him from making contact with anyone. He feels in some obscure way less real, different, from other people, and liable to arouse their antagonism for this reason, and has condemned himself to a lifetime in exile in order to hide his failure in human relations.

His sudden falling in love is all the more astonishing since, at the present moment, he hasn't got even the physical energy required for a normal courtship. But this fact doesn't worry him: without thinking about it consciously, he has allowed the idea of an understanding between them on some other plane to establish itself in his mind, so that there seems no need for him to make any effort.

Although he never tells Luz he loves her or gives any sign of doing so, he's convinced she knows all about it. He even persuades himself that she's about to return his affection – all he has to do is wait. In the meantime, with good-natured indifference, he lets the mother make use of him, acting frequently as her escort.

With Luz herself he is seldom alone. He always recalls with delight a rare occasion when he was able to drive her to a Roman villa above the town, where, on her own for once, she becomes much gayer and more lively, laughing and talking quite easily to him. The outing is a great success altogether, and encourages him to believe that she's fond of him.

And yet, as time goes on, it still never occurs to him to declare his own fondness. He never thinks about marriage at all in a concrete way. Now and then he wishes he could detach the girl from her dominant relative, who appears to hold her in complete subjection. But the wish remains vague, unthought-out, and he does nothing to make it come true, even deriving a certain unacknowledged satisfaction from the thought of her being enslaved.

In due course winter comes to an end. The hillside above the hotel is terraced with olive groves, and under the gnarled old trees wild tulips begin to show swelling buds in the warmer air. There's a sense of life stirring afresh everywhere. Suddenly the wild scarlet tulips burst into dazzling brilliance under the ancient trees. New visitors arrive at the hotel. Chas arrives, a carefree, good-looking young painter, sociable and amusing, who at once becomes popular and a friend of Luke's. The mother promptly deserts her winter companion for this livelier newcomer, who suggests all sorts of picnics and expeditions, which naturally includes Luz.

Now at last the girl seems to be waking up; changing into her more relaxed, more normal self, of which Luke has already caught a brief glimpse. Encouraged by the exhilarating spring atmosphere, she starts talking to people and gradually comes out of her shell altogether. No one now could describe her as listless; she swims and plays tennis all day and dances away half the night.

Both sunshine and moonlight seem magical in that warm, gentle climate. The young man feels, as the tulips flame under the silver trees, that he's watching the revival of a fairy-tale princess who has just been set free from a witch's spell. He is happy simply to see her happy. And as he likes Chas and thinks he's a splendid fellow, doesn't mind her going about with him, feeling she's perfectly safe in his care. Only when the two of them take to disappearing together for whole days, does it strike him that she's spending more and more time with the painter, while he is seeing her less and less.

This of course comes as a horrid shock. When he notices how attentive Chas is, he has a painful sense of urgency, of being abruptly recalled to his conscious self, and his own conduct appears atrocious – how monstrously, madly, presumptuous of him to take everything for granted, doing nothing whatever to gain her affection, instead of exerting himself to the utmost. Now that his relationship with her is in danger, he at last realizes the extent to which it has been a product of his imagination – to translate his romantic dream into instant reality becomes absolutely essential....

But, having arrived at the point where he has got to do something, he hasn't the faintest idea how to deal with the situation, and is assailed, moreover, by a dreadful suspicion that it's already too late and that she has slipped out of his reach.

In desperation, he persuades her to come with him again to the Roman villa (pleasant memories retained from their previous visit make him fancy the place is friendly), in the hope that its beneficent atmosphere will work in his favour and inspire him with the right words. However, nothing of the kind happens. The girl isn't particularly interested in the semi-ruin, and evidently has none of his sentimental liking for it. Nor does she respond to any of the allusions by which he tries to remind her of incidents they have shared during the winter. Seeing this, he grows increasingly agitated, hardly knows what he's saying, and lapses finally into speechless dismay.

Outside is a terrace, overlooking the wide blue sweep of the sea, the town below, and the undulating vista of hilly country planted with grey olive trees, receding in waves to the mountainous background. Wandering out here, oblivious of his distress, she leans against one of the ancient columns, gazing absently at the view, as if she has forgotten that he exists. The warm wind moulds her light dress to the slight curves of her fragile figure, and blows the strange silvery hair back from her smooth white forehead, which is bright in the sun. Her face is lit up too by a new radiance he has never seen there before, and wears a serene, dreaming, half-smiling look which is too much for him to bear.

Rushing up, nearly frantic, he implores her in a distraught voice not to abandon him – to see a little more of him in future. After all, they've known each other the whole winter, whereas Chas.... 'Don't desert your old friends altogether,' he pleads; 'that would be too cruel!'

It seems she has to come back from the far distance to answer; her head slowly turns on the thin, graceful, stemlike neck, her large, limpid eyes bring him gradually into focus, and then she says calmly: 'But I always thought it was my mother you were interested in....'

This practically stuns him. Stupefied by a misapprehension so vast and incredible, he can only stare at her in horrified consternation. *Her* face remains tranquil, her gaze untroubled, as she stands there utterly inaccessible to him. In a sudden frenzy, he starts pouring out a flood of protestations, explanations ... which merely lose themselves in the huge, lovely, indifferent view without in the slightest degree promoting his object. Once more he falters into hopeless silence. Now at last the words 'I love you!' burst out of him of their own accord, but seem to echo in the ensuing silence with a hollow and empty sound, as if uttered by a ghost.

Again she surveys him with those uncannily no-coloured eyes, which darken, dilate and regard him mistrustfully: though the next moment they seem to be looking right through him as if he's not there at all; and soon afterwards return to the panorama and the town below, where Chas is doubtless waiting impatiently.

Total despair overwhelms Luke. Of course he has never succeeded in making himself real to her, cut off, as he always is, by the fatal secret of his unbreakable isolation, different from everyone else in the world. Convinced that she is finally, fatally lost to him, he goes back to the hotel in a daze – almost in a state of collapse – and the following day, hurriedly and almost furtively, departs, without telling anybody beforehand.

*

The sad little story still depressed him as much as ever. Luz was the only human being he'd ever loved. His love for her was the one anchor he had in life; his solitary connection with the living world. Yet now he found himself wondering, as he'd wondered so often before, whether his love was real or just an invention; whether perhaps he was attracted only because she was a glass girl and not quite real, with whom no real contact was possible. Surely, if he'd really been in love, he would have tried harder to get her away from Chas. . . .

Unwilling to acknowledge these familiar doubts, he deliberately transferred his thoughts to the man he had at first liked and admired so much, fearing him later as if he'd belonged to some totally different race of people, threatening to himself. By succeeding where he had so lamentably failed, Chas had demonstrated his triumphant reality, while casting further doubts on his own. Then, after the marriage, his attitude towards the painter had changed again, in response to the latter's friendly invitation to visit them. That was two years ago. During his subsequent travels, he had never ceased to be grateful for the way he'd been welcomed and accepted by both of them at that time, without reference to the past. By their continued friendship, the pair had seemed to give him a share in the human warmth from which his own nature debarred him. In order to suppress the envious sufferings the sight of their happiness caused him, he'd built up a sort of mystique round the marriage, coming to regard their undisguised mutual devotion as something more precious than painful, which he would not have changed if he could.

Nevertheless, he did suffer abominably, and would doubtless continue to do so. In spite of the intervening years, he still hadn't got over the shock of his failure with Luz. Far-reaching psychological consequences of the event were evident in the headaches and insomnia he'd endured ever since, which had forced him to become dependent on tablets he hardly dared swallow because of the dreams they brought – unspeakably hideous, heavenly dreams, inspiring in him horror, shame and ecstatic excitement.

His normal self rejected these dreams even more emphatically than it refused to acknowledge that his true feeling for Luz could be questioned. And now he concentrated all his attention upon the road in an unsuccessful attempt to drive them out of his consciousness altogether. But this evidently was one of the occasions when he had no control over the diabolical images he longed to disown.

Independently going their separate way, his thoughts persistently pursued the atrocious visions, in which the pale girl always appeared as the victim, her tortured delicate body twisted and torn and supremely desirable. Hating himself for indulging in these sadistic fantasies, he desperately struggled to cast them off as he drove; yet he knew all the time he was fighting a losing battle he didn't even whole-heartedly want to win.

Suddenly he had to swerve to avoid a large stone, and the car went into a skid on the icy road. He regained control of it immediately. But in that fragment of time, in an instantaneous flashback, barely interrupting the previous train of ideas, his inner eye recognized a strange upright boulder standing alone in a field like some primitive unfinished sculpture, which, as a small boy, he'd been told the glaciers had deposited there in the course of their slow retreat after the ice-age. White flakes were starting to fly at the windscreen out of the dark; he just had time to suppose that the association of ice and snow had recalled this long-forgotten memory, before his thoughts reverted wholly to the earlier theme they had never entirely left.

Giving up the struggle at this point, he surrendered voluptuously to the shameful pleasure stirring his blood. The warmth in the car contributed to his warm sense of well-being as he looked out at a desolate waste, upon which snow was steadily falling. . . .

The dead white landscape is broken only by a few blackish, twisted tree-stumps or distant boulders, and one quite near him, which appears to have been roughly hacked into the crude shape of a man with hugely enlarged genitals and rudimentary limbs; to which the girl's trembling naked figure is bound.

The watcher stares, fascinated, never taking his eyes off her. She does not look at him. Her head is turned away slightly but not enough to prevent him from seeing her wide eyes, dilated with terror, fixed on a glistening white circular wall of ice, of which she is the centre, as it slowly approaches.

Suddenly the pace of the advance must quicken, though he doesn't actually see this, for now the outer fringe of the ice cliff has already reached her . . . already set, hard as concrete, over her feet and her thin ankles.

She throws her head back, turning it wildly from side to side in the only movement of which she is still capable, her whole delicate body convulsed, writhing frantically in its bonds.

Uncontrollable delight flaring in all his veins, the onlooker sees the ice mount implacably to her calves ... to her knees ... hears her thin, long-drawn, agonized cry as it finally climbs to her thighs ... forcing them apart. ...

The delectable, detestable vision, fading into present reality, immediately started to slide out of his memory: and he saw all at once that he had crossed another road without noticing it. He was about to turn back in search of a signpost when he changed his mind and looked more attentively at what was visible of the scene in front. The headlights revealed something vaguely familiar about it, and he decided to keep on up the hill; he might be on the right road after all. Only a few moments later, the strong lights dramatically lit up a deserted farmhouse he was almost certain he recognized as the place where they'd stopped for a picnic lunch when he was here before. But now, in midwinter, the ground white with snow, things looked so different ... besides, he'd only had such a brief glimpse. ... In the end he wasn't sure that it really was the same spot.

*

The shadows of the trees move on, leaving the bank where they ate their lunch in full sun. Luke moves a few steps higher up to sit in the shade of an old pear tree growing beside the door of the empty farm. Chas gets up too and goes down to the car on the road below, extracting his sketchbook from it and waving carelessly, before disappearing into the dense greenery of the beech woods.

Luz is the only one who still lies, relaxed, in the sunshine; while Luke, chewing a grass stalk, sits watching her. He's very conscious that this is the first time they have been left alone together, and wonders if she is too – if so, she makes no sign. Motionless, her hands clasped over her eyes, she might be asleep. The slight curves of her almost childish body are clearly visible through her thin dress, which is sleeveless, so that he can see the tiny bright beads of sweat in her armpits against the slight darkness and roughness of the shaved skin. Almost as if to himself, he says now: 'I had to come and make certain that you were happy.'

She can't be asleep, for she reacts instantly, twisting round to face him in a strained, tense, sprawling position, while he tries to reassure her by going on lightly: 'Don't worry – I shan't bother you any more. Now that I've seen just how happy you are, I can vanish again into the great trackless swamps.'

But the effect is nil. She only stares at him silently in that odd twisted posture that would be ungainly in another person, supporting her weight on her hands, her bare arms widely spread. The abruptness of her movement has disarranged her dress, exposing one leg right up to the thigh, and he takes it as a measure of her disturbance that no instinctive modesty prompts her to pull down her skirt. The low-necked dress hangs away from her body so that he, sitting slightly above her, can see the shadows between her breasts and even the small protruberances of the nipples, which in conjunction with the bareness of her arms and legs produces the momentary illusion that she is naked before him.

The pupils of her eyes have grown dark and enormous, expanding wider and wider. He watches these hugely dilated eyes deepen into two black bottomless pools, which amalgamate finally, and engulf the victim's pale fragile body in spite of its struggles. Her head comes up once, mouth wide open to scream or gasping for air. But before she can make a sound or take a breath, the black flood pours down her throat, choking her ... obliterating her altogether....

The slight breeze which has been rustling the beeches expires suddenly; heat and sunshine become excessive. Unbearably hot all at once, Luke unfastens his shirt – his jacket already lies on the grass beside him. At the same time he hears the distant thud of the painter's returning footsteps, followed by the most unexpected sound of his own voice: 'Remember that if you're ever in any trouble I'll always come back to you.'

The words are so unpremeditated that he seems to have no foreknowledge of them. They might almost have been spoken by someone else, in that low, intense tone, unfamiliar to him.

Breaking her immobility though not her silence, his companion jumps up. For a second he sees her eyes glitter among long flickering lashes before she turns away, and, keeping her face averted, collects the debris of the picnic, and carries it down to the car.

He can hardly stop himself following her. But the husband is already quite close, mopping his brow as he approaches, sitting down beside him under the pear tree – now he can't go without being pointedly rude.

Not hearing a word that's said to him, he sits on, hoping only that Chas doesn't notice his preoccupation, or the way his eyes keep straying towards the car.

Not that Luz is to be seen down there. She seems to have wandered off by herself, and doesn't reappear until it's time to drive home; when she insists on sitting alone at the back of the car, and doesn't open her mouth the whole way.

*

The road climbed steeply between high banks, as if he were in a cutting between giant earthworks, or crawling along like a beetle between huge stones. His knowledge of the hidden devastation around him made the night seem ominous. A lingering self-disgust had resulted in his unadmitted fear of the dark and its dangers, as though he were surrounded by threatening secrets.

Suddenly an opening showed ahead in the towering banks, the approach to a group of buildings, clotted above in a menacing, fortlike mass. This forbidding outline, a dream-distortion of the row of cottages he half remembered, also brought back a dim recollection. But then, catching sight of collapsing walls and empty window-holes like wide-open screaming mouths, he decided not to trust his memory, since such deterioration was hardly possible in the time he had been away.

There could be no doubt, however, about the tall single tree he saw growing in a triangle of frosted grass, which must be the chestnut they used to sit under when they came to the village pub for a drink. It was unmistakable. Or would have been, but for his inexplicable conviction that *this* was a dead tree, no more able to produce the deep shade he remembered than the nondescript semi-ruin behind it could produce a drink.

Confused by these half-recognitions and contradictions, he still wasn't sure that he had come to the right place: though there couldn't be many roads which ended, as this one did, in three sides of a triangle and went no further, as if there were no way of reaching the top of the hill. Taking a chance, he made for a matted blackness of ivy and evergreens; and, sure enough, the headlights picked out the whitish chalky gleam of the lane leading to his friends' house, worming its way through the dark tangle. A moment later he again wondered whether he'd been mistaken, when the track became almost impassable, a narrow deeply rutted tunnel between untended hedges that met overhead. As there was nowhere to turn, he was obliged to keep on somehow; and suddenly a fresh recollection emerged – if he really was on the right track, the next bend would reveal a gate where the beech woods began.

Yes, there it was, a five-bar gate as broken-down as he'd by now come to expect. And there too, some distance beyond it, was his destination, at which he looked in astonishment, not because of its dilapidated air (he'd begun to take this decomposing night-world for granted), but because he wasn't expecting to see it yet, having made no allowance for the much longer vistas afforded by the leafless trees.

Instead of being cheered by the sight, he was overcome by gloom and despondency. Had it been possible to turn back here he would have done so; as it was not, he had to go on, but decided not to enter the house when he got there. All of a sudden he felt extraordinarily tired, as if he'd been driving in the dark for an eternity on these winding, treacherous, slippery country roads. The headache he'd hardly noticed before thrust itself on his attention. He ought to have brought some aspirins with him. He was rarely without them, and wondered how he'd come to overlook them today. Well, he could ask Chas for some. But he no longer wanted to see his friends. The fact was, in his present condition, he couldn't bear to see them so happy together. But neither, apparently, could he bear not to see them, for instead of turning the car at the top of the hill, he drove in at the gate, propped open by heavy stones – one of its hinges had gone, he observed in passing.

Giant yews, centuries old and of vast diameter, loomed over him, massive, threatening, looking substantial as black towers. He'd always disliked yews ever since he was a boy, running through forbidden coverts to meet a friend, when one of these black churchyard trees had obstructed him, and he'd been captured and punished by the angry gamekeeper.

His main attention focused elsewhere. The thought at the back of his mind scarcely registered that, ever since that remote occasion, the same tall black forbidding shape had stood before every human being he tried to approach, blocking his way, prohibiting any contact.

He stopped in front of the porch, and for a startled second had the impression that the wall beside it was crumbling; until he saw how massed invasive creepers produced this illusion, their thick entwined strands matted together and resembling chaotic piles of masonry in the glare of the car lights. Like all the other buildings he'd passed, the house was dark and appeared empty, not a chink of light showing anywhere. Of course his friends must have gone away. He jumped at this simple explanation of the surrounding neglect, at the same time perfectly aware that it didn't account for the widespread desolation all along his route. The deserted scene brought on another wave of depression, and he was on the point of driving away when the door of the house was noisily flung open by someone he couldn't see.

It most certainly wasn't Luz. He supposed Chas must be standing there in the dark porch, but he couldn't be sure that it wasn't someone else of similar build, who seemed to radiate violence and resentment in a way that was most unlike his amiable friend. However, he could no longer doubt his identity when he came right up to the car and looked into his face, saying: 'So it really *is* you'.

The man sounded more astonished than pleased, and gave a short, disconcerting laugh before going on: 'A minute ago I was thinking of you as thousands of miles away on the other side of the world; and here you are suddenly, on my doorstep.'

'I've just got back,' Luke replied. 'I meant to arrive much earlier – to give you a surprise – but I lost my way.' Puzzled by the alteration in his friend's manner, which indeed could hardly be described as friendly, he suddenly realized that, though he'd suppressed his own negative feelings, he had all the time felt an intermittent uneasiness in their relations. In confused disappointment, he continued: 'I know it's too late to drop in at this time of night – I'll go now that I've seen you.' He put the car in gear, but that was all; he was powerless to leave without seeing Luz, or at least hearing about her. He tried vainly to look into the house, which seemed to be all in darkness.

'Oh, you surprised me all right,' Chas said drily. His voice, malicious or mocking hinted at something that was not clear.

Luke now felt definitely rebuffed, and was prevented from leaving on the spot only by his desire for news of Luz. As it already seemed too late for him to ask after her directly, he repeated: 'I'll be off now . . .'

'Nonsense!' The other suddenly changed his tone, speaking as if he were smiling, though no smile appeared on his face. 'Of course you're not going. Come along in!' He sounded hearty, but still there was no real friendliness about him; it was more as if he were imitating his old cordiality.

Not knowing what to make of his odd behaviour, wondering whether he could be drunk, Luke got out of the car and let himself be propelled into the porch as if sleep-walking.

'Well, here we go again!' All at once becoming boisterous, the painter took his arm and pulled him through the door, which promptly blew shut behind them. Equally confused by his changeability and the dark interior, the visitor felt trapped. He couldn't recall how the rooms were arranged, the hall seemed larger than he remembered. 'Mind your head on that beam!' he heard. But he wasn't warned about a forgotten step down, and stumbled into the living-room, which also seemed larger, the feeble light leaving the corners in darkness and all detail obscure. A faint warmth still came from the open hearth. Chas kicked the remains of the fire ineffectually, then piled on heavy logs, which almost extinguished its last few sparks. 'Stay here and warm up while I scout round and see what I can find. . . .' His voice trailed off into the dark silence outside the door.

Luke automatically rearranged the logs to give them a chance to catch, noting dust on the mantelpiece as he straightened up. He grew extremely uncomfortable looking round the room he knew so well, which now had the strangeness of something remembered out of a dream. Not only Chas himself, but the whole house, was different, its former tranquil happy atmosphere replaced by something related to the deterioration outside. He discerned a slight untidiness, a faint air of neglect, the room made an uncared-for impression he couldn't reconcile with his fastidious glass girl – what was she doing in this ambience? Where was she? Why hadn't Chas mentioned her? The omission could hardly be accidental. . . .

The fire had started to flicker feebly. Suddenly the logs burst into flames, just as the man he was thinking about reappeared, holding a bottle of wine. In the sudden blaze of light his changed face gave Luke a shock. It looked quite different, almost a stranger's, scored by deep lines, the full, rather sensuous lips tensed and narrowed. How much of this was due to the leaping flames? A generally slightly disintegrated appearance, as if the whole athletic muscular body had been infected by the decay outside, must be an illusion. . . . Realizing how he was staring, he extricated himself from these speculations in time to hear the words 'Well, here's to our friendship!' uttered with a sort of phoney exuberance, while the speaker, pouring out the wine carelessly as though he were drunk, or pretending to be drunk, emptied his glass at one gulp.

Struck by a curious unpleasant sense of falseness pervading his behaviour, Luke wondered uncomfortably what the man's motive could be in putting on this act. He himself felt more uneasy than ever, oppressed by the whole situation, unable to fix his attention on what was said. He didn't attempt to keep pace with the other man's drinking, and was surprised, when the bottle was pushed towards him, to see that his glass was empty; he had no recollection of drinking, and covered it with his hand, not wanting to drink any more. His headache was getting worse all the time, he was dead tired, and if he hadn't had such a craving to see Luz, he would have made an excuse to leave there and then. Yet, when his companion urged him to drink up, he allowed his glass to be refilled out of sheer inertia.

Chas sat watching him without speaking, in apparent amusement. The greenish eyes at least were unchanged; but what were they seeing? Not what they used to see of him, Luke was sure; they seemed to look at him like a stranger's; like the eyes of someone who hardly knew him. Suddenly they started to wink, darting sly, equivocal glances in his direction, accompanying the words 'It's funny, you know – you and I sitting here like this....'

Not understanding, suspecting malice, he asked with defensive sharpness: 'What's funny about it?' But immediately afterwards lost all interest, overcome by the heat of the fire, which seemed to have reached an unbearable intensity. He tried to push his chair away, but it wouldn't move. He had to be satisfied with throwing his overcoat back as far as possible on his shoulders. To take it off, he felt, would commit him to staying; and he was determined to go as soon as he'd found out about Luz. It occurred to him that Chas must be keeping quiet about her deliberately, just to spite him. But he was again distracted by an unpleasant physical sensation, his forgotten hunger reasserting itself as an interior void, where the wine he had drunk was queasily sloshing about. Protestingly, his stomach emitted a dismal growl; the need to stabilize it became so acute that he had to ask if he could have something to eat.

'But of course.' Chas got up, then stood looking at him with a distinctly spiteful expression over the table on which stood the now empty bottle. 'It really is damned funny, the two of us drinking together.' He laughed shortly, a humourless, obnoxious sound.

Luke, taken aback, said, in acute embarrassment: 'I don't know what you mean . . .'

'Think it out, then!' The other had already left the room: which next moment was echoing with his shouts, barely muffled by the intervening wall. 'Luz! Luz! 'What the hell are you doing? Come down at once and get us some food!' Silence followed, broken only by his heavy steps pounding upstairs.

Luke, who had jumped up in alarm, was astounded to hear him use this angry, abusive, peremptory tone to the girl he had adored – with whom he'd been absolutely infatuated two years before. Hurrying to the door, he stood listening, wondering whether he ought to follow and be ready to protect her if necessary – his first impression of the man's violence seemed to have been correct. But all remained quiet. It wasn't for him to interfere, he decided, retiring instead to his chair, where he sat for an unmeasured period, holding his aching head in his hands, quite stupefied by the heat and this last most unexpected change in the situation.

When he looked up, the fire had reached its hottest, incandescent stage, so that he received the wave of intense heat full in the face, like the blast from a furnace. For a second it made him feel dizzy, the room began to revolve around him, then gradually slowed to a standstill. His head still ached abominably, and his coat had again slipped forward – his first deliberate act was to push it as far back as he could with both hands.

'Why don't you take it off?'

Though he instantly recognized the soft voice, to answer it seemed beyond him. Nor did Luz appear to expect a reply, quietly putting bread, butter and cheese on the table in front of him, followed by three bowls of soup.

'Is that the best you can do?'

Without even his fake geniality now, the painter sounded quarrelsome and vindictive. Luke was again almost dazed by astonishment at the incredible hostility he had developed towards his wife. It simply wasn't to be believed... he must be dreaming... none of this could be really happening....

Nobody spoke as they started eating; the host's heavy silence effectively put a stop to all conversation. He'd produced another bottle of wine, and, uncorking it, signed to Luz to hold out her glass, his big, strong hands looking brutal by contrast with the almost transparent one she extended obediently. Luke couldn't stop watching her, fascinated by that brittle-looking hand and wrist... it was as if he'd forgotten her extreme fragility... yet knew his inmost self never for one moment forgot her frail, delicate, victim's body. She remote, listless, as when he first met her, sitting with bent head within her shower of strange white shining hair, pale as an albino's. He tried to will her to look at him, but couldn't even induce her to raise her eyes. She hadn't spoken to him except for her one question; had showed not the slightest surprise at his sudden arrivals. He began to feel that she too had become a stranger.

Did he still love her? The old question arose, mechanically circling round his tired brain. Had he *ever* loved her? Hadn't it always been just a pretence, as he'd never done anything about it?

For a moment he put his hand in front of his eyes, feeling weary, muddled and sad. His headache was starting to have a confusing effect: he longed to be out in the air; why didn't he get up and go? But, much as he wanted to escape from this impossible silence that went on and on, he didn't like to make a move without even knowing whether the meal was supposed to be over. His soup-bowl was empty; but Luz had hardly touched hers. His eyes went from one silent figure to the other, and his confusion intensified; he felt more than ever that he must be dreaming. It was quite beyond his powers to identify these speechless strangers with the friends he had come to see.

*

Alone in the living-room, Luke sits on the step of the wide open window, facing into the summer garden. Like all the others, this last day of his visit is warm and sunny. Everything here is already idealized in his mind. He feels a boundless grateful affection for these two precious, wonderful people, who, by being his friends, have for the first time in his life brought him into the warmth of human companionship. Lost in a sort of day-dream, he is sitting so still half outside the room, that Luz doesn't notice him when she comes in with a big bunch of flowers and starts arranging them in a tall jug. She is singing quietly to herself, and continues to be unaware of his motionless presence, starting violently when he finally turns to smile at her, saying: 'That settles it...'

'Settles what?' The anxiety that comes so easily to her face dilates and darkens her big eyes.

Still half dreaming, he doesn't realize how much he has startled her. For the moment his thoughts are far off in a tropical forest with his favourite animals, the weird, man-sized, singing lemurs called the Indris, supposed to be the origin of the legend of the dog-headed man. Very few people have ever seen these almost extinct creatures, and fewer still have heard their uncanny song, which has a tremendous fascination for him. He explains now how she and Chas remind him of the Indris, because they too are kind and loving, gentle and playful, and live together so happily here in the trees. 'And now that I've heard you sing, the resemblance is complete.'

Charmed by his notion, he isn't seeing her objectively, although his gaze is fixed on her slender figure, outlined in its light dress against the shadowy room. It's not the same dress she wore at the picnic, he notices vagely, but one very like it, sleeveless and with rather a low neck.

'You heard me singing?'

If he was attending, he'd surely wonder why she sounds so horrified, and turns her head aside like a little girl caught in the act of some childish misdeed; the fact being that she was singing for joy because he'll so soon be gone. Besides, she always has a deeper sense of guilt in relation to him which she doesn't understand – she would never have come in here if she'd guessed he might be in the room, and she is trying feverishly to think how to escape without seeming rude.

'Do you often sing to yourself? I've never heard you before.'

'Only when I'm specially happy.' Having suddenly realized that she needn't worry as he can't possibly know what's going on in her mind, her face lightens and she smiles almost mischievously.

His thoughts are still half with the lemurs. He doesn't ask why she's so happy just now, but begins to talk about the creatures he's so fond of, and their idyllic, innocent life in the jungle, at peace with all its inhabitants, eating flower petals in the tree-tops, caressing each other, and singing their melodious, unearthly songs. The strange beasts are almost an obsession of his, their eerie voices enchant him. He loves speaking about them and has often described them to her before. But no amount of description of their endearing ways has any effect on the inexplicable aversion she's always felt towards them and their unnatural music. Wishing he'd talk about something else, she hardly listens as she finishes arranging her flowers, until he exclaims: 'I love you and I love the Indris ... nobody, nothing, else in the world – it's perfect that you should be like them!'

His dreamy state has passed into one almost of exaltation. He's not at all clear as to his own meaning, and certainly doesn't realize what he has just said. His everyday common sense would never countenance such an extraordinary statement, which his hearer can't be expected to understand.

She is, in fact, gazing at him in amazement. Anxiety, always as close to her as her shadow, has returned to her face. Again she wants to get away from him, and, merely saying that she's going to pick ferns in the wood for another floral arrangement, she steps quickly past him, out into the shady garden.

He neither moves nor speaks, staring after her almost as if in a trance, watching her recede, the light lingering on her pale hair and bare arms and legs with a faint greenish tinge from the surrounding woodland. The secluded garden is deep in the beach woods, hidden away from the world in silence and secrecy, isolated by the countless great trees pressing close on all sides, their ancient enormous trunks ranked close together like walls... like impassable prison walls... the dense massive foliage pierced here and there by only a few small scattered rings of light, which give no idea of how the sun is blazing down on the world outside....

The tremendous ocean of leaves, encroaching everywhere on the small open space, fills the air with a green liquid transparency, and this fluid greenery arches up in colossal waves, overhanging and threatening the house... collapses and surges forward in a vast green tide, overwhelming everything... sweeping the girl away....

She turns once; he sees her dilated victim's eyes gaze wildly, imploringly, at him, before she is engulfed by the assaulting flood.

*

Luke pressed his hand to his forehead, repeating the gesture after a pause, in the hope that someone would see that he was in pain and offer to get him some aspirin. But though he kept his fingers pressed on his eyelids until fiery flashes appeared on his retina, nobody took any notice.

A paralysing lassitude enveloped him now. Above all things he wanted to go. He knew it must be very late and that he *ought* to go. But, checked and chilled by the prospect of driving all the way back to town in the icy, hostile darkness, he stayed huddled up in his chair, one hand over his eyes. He was half asleep when he heard: 'And what's brought you back so suddenly from your travels?'

Looking up, he saw that Chas had risen and was standing above him; and was instantly shocked wide awake by meeting his penetrating, perspicacious, unfriendly glance in one of those revealing glimpses of another person which infrequently, disconcertingly, pierced his isolation, disclosing the obscure, dangerous, misleading territory of human relations. How much the man must dislike him.

'You were sent for, I take it. Such superlative timing could hardly be a coincidence.' This was said in a much lower voice, inaudible probably to the third person present. The green glinting eyes snapped maliciously at him out of the virile, vicious, flame-distorted face. As he only stared back blankly, the low voice added: 'I refer, of course, to the superb timing of your reappearance.'

Luke was far too taken aback to answer, unable to marshal his scattered wits into any semblance of order, not even grasping what the words meant. They struck him as totally inexplicable, incomprehensible, uttered in that quick, knowing, spiteful undertone which seemed to deal secret blows he was too numbed to feel yet, seeing only the sharp green eyes, fixed on him with dislike, with disgust almost. They vanished suddenly, the painter turned away to search for something on the shelves by the door, then swung round again with a record in his hand. 'Let's have some music if you've got nothing to say.'

'Oh no, Chas – not the singing! I can't stand it!'

Luke got a fresh shock, hearing this sudden outcry from the girl who'd been silent so long.

Luz seemed to know that her protest would be ignored, for she jumped up, exclaiming 'I won't listen to it!' and made a dash for the door. Before she got there, her husband's big hand seized her in a policeman's grip: grinning maliciously but saying nothing, he held her helplessly tethered to him, while his other hand put on the record and started the mechanism. His prolonged grasp must have been hurting her thin wrist, for she kept trying to struggle free, her face contorted in a childish grimace of pain.

Luke drew in his breath sharply, clenching his fists, but did nothing to help her. The record was circling with a low whirr that merged with the sighing of the wind in the trees; the soft, soporific murmur reminded him of nights spent in this house, when he'd seemed to fall asleep to the sound of a quietly breathing sea. His mesmerized gaze never left the slight form of the victim, whose hair shimmered round her head in a silvery cloud as she twisted and turned. Unconsciously moistening his dry lips with the tip of his tongue, he leaned forward, hungrily staring, thrilled and tormented by the strained, unfamiliar poses her slight body assumed in its futile struggles.

Suddenly, without warning, the subdued murmur filling his head swelled to a wailing that seemed actually inside it, welling up louder and louder, pounding against his temples.

Somehow he eventually recognized in these discordant sounds a distortion of the magic song of the Indris, a record of which he had left with his friends as a parting gift after his last visit. Yet they were totally unlike the enchanted music he loved. The lemurs' singing had always seemed to him not of this world, so that he'd come to identify it with another and happier life, regarding it as the symbol of all that he held most precious ... of a world where intelligence and affection were cherished, and destructiveness and cruelty had no place.

Now the lovely, unearthly melody was transformed into these hideous discords, harshly insisting that all the things he most valued were irretrievably lost, that destruction had after all triumphed, and that *this* was the only world. The message was far too painful to him ... he couldn't bear it ... wanting only to escape from the atrocious dissonance which had replaced the harmonies he adored.

Without noticing any transition, he found himself out in the hall, which was dark and extremely cold after the heat of the fire. No one had followed him and the door was shut. But, though the uncanny singing was muted here, he could still hear how horribly it had changed ... to get right away, out of earshot, remained his sole object. Pulling his overcoat round him and buttoning it, he groped his way towards the door to the outside world, thinking only of making a quick escape from the sounds penetrating the other door behind him; while the excruciating cacophony vibrated inside his skull, rising and falling with his erratic pulse.

To his profound relief, a blessed silence fell suddenly. He paused to listen, half expecting the hideous noise to burst out again. However, all he heard was the soft rustling of trees in the wind outside; or so he thought, until he realized that this sound was indoors and quite near him – was, in fact, the rustle of a woman's dress.

He looked round and saw Luz coming towards him, her slenderness outlined against a dim light behind. She was her usual self, perfectly calm and quiet, her pale hair smoothly combed. Of her recent struggles there was no sign, which puzzled and briefly disturbed him. Was he imagining things? And if so, which version was real? So far he hadn't noticed what she was wearing: but because he himself felt cold out here, even in his thick overcoat, he now observed the short sleeves and rather low neck of her simple dress, which was very much like those she used to wear in the summer, and looked scarcely warmer.

As she approached, the feeble light revealed her protruding collar-bones, showing deep pits of shadow at the base of her neck. Her thinness seemed exaggerated by the uncertain illumination... she looked far too thin... emaciated, almost, like a famine victim. He was not unaware of the pathos of her appearance, but when she extended her hand, his attention instantly became riveted on the projecting wrist-bones – with a spasm of the old hateful joy, he feels he could snap them between his finger and thumb....

Snow is falling heavily, and on the dead white background her naked flesh is milk or ivory coloured... except where the cords binding her wrists have bitten in deeply, leaving them encircled by angry red savage rings. The steadily falling snow encloses the two of them in its lonely tent, settles in big white flakes on her shrinking body, whitening still further the strange bright hair falling over her breasts, in which she seems to be trying pathetically to clothe herself....

'I've brought you some aspirin....

For a second, the low voice had no meaning for him; he seemed to be looking down at two exceptionally large and solid snowflakes. Then recognizing the two tablets in the palm of her hand, he scooped them up awkwardly, faintly embarrassed by the dissolving image he was already forgetting... which, by the time he had swallowed them and returned the glass of water she'd handed him, had been obliterated from his mind without trace. The urgent need to escape once more in control, he went on to the door and out to his car, hardly noticing that she stood crushed against the side of the porch as though afraid to come any further.

She said nothing until he had climbed into the driver's seat, when she called out 'Do you remember...?' so softly that the last words of the sentence failed to reach him. Since she neither moved nor repeated her question, he saw that he'd have to get out of the car to discover the end of it. But, at that moment, wild horses couldn't have dragged him back to the house; so he pretended not to have heard her at all, and, after several attempts, managed to start the engine.

The car began to move; he turned, waving goodbye, and, as the headlights passed over her face, he saw it appear to break up into conflicting planes as if she were crying. He forgot the effect at once, for a man's tremendous arm, black and swollen with muscle like an executioner's, suddenly shot out of the doorway, and a huge, brutal hand gripped her with such violence that she swayed and started to fall. . . . Simultaneously and abruptly, everything vanished – the giant arm and hand, the bright collapsing head and frail shoulders, melting at the same time into each other and into utter blackness, until nothing at all remained visible.

Luke drove on, deciding he must have imagined the gigantic hand – nothing so fantastic could possibly have been real. Besides, his recollection of it was already blurred and beyond the periphery of normal perception. He was passing the yew trees' ominous black towers when the muted slam of the house door made him glance back, though without realizing what the sound implied. Still nothing whatsoever was to be seen behind him; neither the two figures, the trees nor the house itself . . . and his head seemed correspondingly empty.

From then onwards absolute darkness encompassed him, out of which flurries of snow flew intermittently, so that he faced a confused white whirling wall, and drove for the rest of the time in a vast black vacancy.

*

Arriving so late at the garage, he finds that the lift isn't working, and having put his car at the top, he has to walk all the way down the ramp, round and round endless, windowless, claustrophobic spirals between concrete walls devoid of relief or colour. However, as soon as he reaches the street, the memory of the garage evaporates in the freezing air, and so does his headache. He doesn't feel tired any more.

It isn't snowing at the moment, though a deep, unmarked layer of pure white covers street and pavement. There are no pedestrians, no traffic, the snowbound city lies deserted, in the icy small hours. He turns the corner, expecting to confront the entrance to his hotel; but instead finds himself in a street he doesn't know.

The lights burns indifferently in the white vacancy of the long, straight street, stretching into the distance. The traffic-lights at the intersections keep up their useless changes; the spotless snow reflects in incessant sequence a faint red glow, an orange glow, a green glow, reverting to orange and red. Every window has the same white trimming; the same depth of white is piled in every doorway. All the houses look exactly alike with their white decoration. The snow, the emptiness, the distant constellations of coloured lights, winking on and off simultaneously, create a confusing sameness, bewildering to the eye. There is nothing to distinguish this street from any other, or one house from the next. Yet he seems to know where he's going, and walks briskly, the snow crunching under his feet.

Here is an entrance from which the snow has been swept – a striking distinction in this white waste land of similarity – and he goes in without hesitation. An attendant escorts him to a curtained door, enjoining silence, his finger on his lips. The door opens at once from the other side, admitting Luke to a small, crowded theatre, lit only from the stage, where a solitary figure is dancing. The attendant has gone back to the entry, and whoever let him in, instead of waiting to show him to a seat, has already vanished. He can't see where there's an empty place among the rows of crouching, faceless, identical figures, and decides to stay where he is until the lights go up. Although right at the side, he can see very well, being so near the stage.

The blonde dancer looks half starved, her bones seem on the verge of perforating her delicate skin. Yet her body is graceful, though hardly likely to appeal to patrons of a late-night show, since its curves have an almost childish fragility. Only the torso moves, her feet remain trapped in a tiny circle midstage. Perhaps in an attempt to compensate for what is lacking in mature sexual allure, a dead white spotlight paints her flesh with intense, melodramatic shadows, and in this hard, strong light her slender limbs appear actually frangible. The mutilations inflicted by the black shadows support the impression of helpless surrender and dread produced by her miming, showing her as the victim of some archaic ceremony, about to culminate in human sacrifice.

With unexpected abruptness the dance reaches its climax. Her ankles bound presumably, she is still immobolized from the waist down, though she throws her head back and twists the upper part of her body so violently that a faint sheen of moisture starts to glisten on the smooth flesh... her mouth opens wide in a soundless scream....

Too absorbed in the dancer to notice whether there's any applause, Luke sees that she looks completely exhausted as she leaves the stage. Already she is in deep shadow, receding towards total darkness in the wings, out of which comes an enormous hand, which clamps itself over her mouth, while another seizes one brittle-looking ankle and tugs her forward. Without a sound she topples into the dark and is instantly devoured by it. . . .

3

THE position is not uncomfortable, except for the cord to ensure that she's posed correctly, exactly as she was yesterday, which Chas has tied rather too tight. She doesn't complain about it, vaguely hoping that if she submits to everything, without ever making trouble, he will love her again and her happiness will return. This is not even entirely believed; and certainly not thought out rationally in an adult fashion. Her mind works more like that of a little girl, obedient and docile, who has nevertheless unaccountably lost the love of a grown-up person and feels it must be her own fault, without being able to imagine how it possibly can be.

She adores him and would do anything for him. It's such a small thing to act as his model; all through the summer she has gladly posed for him in the nude. It's only now, in the midst of this exceptionally severe winter, that she gets so terribly cold and can hardly bear to keep still. Already her arms and legs have turned numb; though this doesn't prevent her from feeling the cord bite viciously into her flesh. She wonders unhappily what the time is. It must be long past the period when she's supposed to have a few minutes' rest. Chas often forgets the rest periods these days, and she doesn't like to remind him. Making a great effort to stop thinking about herself, she turns her eyes to the window. Although it's far too dark to see anything outside, she seems to catch a dissolving glimpse of white moths swarming against the glass – it must be snowing again.

Snow.... Perhaps because she's always lived before in warm climates, snow has a peculiar effect on her, like something supernatural – like some kind of magic, fascinating but dangerous. Even the thought of it makes her feel strange.... Suddenly she's acutely aware of her numb frozen limbs and can't suppress a convulsive shudder, which shakes her from head to foot.

'Keep still, can't you?' The man at the easel sounds angry, then looks at his watch and exclaims: 'Good God! we ought to have stopped long ago – why on earth didn't you tell me?' Still seeming more annoyed than sorry, he unties her quickly, his expression an odd mixture of exasperation and guilt, afterwards wrapping her in a blanket, keeping his arm round her while he kicks open the doors of the stove.

Relaxing against him for a blissful moment she leans on his strength. But all at once he abruptly seems to forget all about her, withdrawing both his support and his attention completely and at the same time, so that she recovers her balance only at the last moment. Meanwhile he has gone back to stand in front of his easel, staring at the canvas as though she no longer existed.

*

Husband and wife sit facing each other across a table, on which is the remains of their evening meal. They have finished eating some minutes ago, but don't move. Neither do they speak. It is to be felt that the silence in the room has lasted a long time. The man is unconscious of it, deeply preoccupied, perhaps still thinking about his work. The girl too seems to be thinking of something else – or of nothing at all – and to be exhausted, ill, miserable, or suffering from some neurosis, sitting there in a drooping posture, her head resting on her hand.

Presently she gets up and, still without saying a word, collects the used plates and cutlery on a tray, and carries it out to the kitchen. As if he has been waiting for this move of hers, Chas stands up then and leaves the room by a different door. Returning to find him gone, Luz looks troubled: hesitating a moment, she goes after him; but suddenly stops dead in the passage outside a closed door through which comes the sound she detests above all others. What she hears is a kind of music – non-human voices singing together in rhythm, rising and falling in successive regular waves, sinking to a murmur while the next wave builds up its mounting volume, which culminates in a prolonged chord, sounding to her more like a howl.

It is of course the recorded song of the Indris, left here by Luke as a parting gift. How she hates it! How she hates everything connected with those uncanny lemurs! If only he hadn't come to stay here and talked so much about them! She doesn't know why she has always felt so antagonistic to the weird creatures, to which he once compared her. She has always thought the comparison grotesque and outrageous, but now it seems to be something worse — she's appalled by the mere idea of a possible resemblance between her and the infernal singers, whose voices continue to bombard her ears with what sound like atrocious discords, until she feels like howling herself. Yes, her nerves are exacerbated to such an extent that she could actually lift up her chin and howl like a dog each time the sound-waves assault her; and her face contracts each time as with the pain of a physical blow.... There's something altogether terrifying and unearthly about the sound.

Why is Chas, who has never shown any interest in music before, so enchanted by this record. that he listens to it day and night? He seems absolutely spellbound by its atrocious rhythms... at this moment she really believes the music has some diabolical magic power, which will finally be her undoing.

At last it comes to an end, and she takes a deep breath of relief. But immediately the hateful dissonance is renewed. To hear the record again is more than she can endure; in her distraught state she simply can't stand it. Quite beside herself, she jumps at the door, flings it open, rushes frantically into the room and stops the mechanism so forcibly and abruptly that the voices cease on a high wailing note of anguish.

'What do you think you're doing, bursting in here like a maniac? Have you gone off your head?' The man stands up, rather red in the face, but otherwise calm.

She, on the contrary, has lost every atom of self-control. Tears springing out of her eyes unchecked, she accuses him incoherently of playing the record so often simply because he knows it upsets her and that she loathes the wretched Indris. 'You used not to care about music so much,' she sobs, childishly brushing away with her fingers the falling tears she doesn't attempt to hide.

'Do you expect me to sit in dead silence, like a deaf-mute?' Enormous suppressed resentment comes out in his hostile tone. 'You never open your mouth these days, and I can't ask anyone here because you're so damned unsociable....' His indignation increasing, he works himself into a rage at the thought of all he has to put up with. 'You'd like to keep me shut up alone with you in solitary confinement, I know.... But you won't succeed... if you go on like this you're much more likely to lose me altogether.' A scowling glance accompanies this threat, and he strides out of the room, slamming the door behind him.

The weeping girl doesn't try to follow him or call him back, but sinks down on the floor by his chair and buries her face in the cushions, sobbing without restraint. Happiness is not for her – she has always known it. For a time she enjoyed it illegitimately and so she feels guilty . . . though really it's Luke she feels guilty about, heaven knows why . . . she's certainly never given him the least encouragement. She only wanted to forget all about him, and was shocked when his visit was first suggested. But Chas, laughing, had said she musn't live entirely in a dream-world and shut everyone out. That was during the time of her lost happiness, when his love had built round her a protective wall, which for a brief period had seemed unassailable, indestructible, just the two of them together inside, everything intimate and secure. She'd felt so blissfully safe and happy in those days. What strength, what confidence he had instilled into her. As long as he loved her, she could laugh at the world outside. With him she had even laughed at her domineering mother, who in the past had reduced her to nothing. It had been so miraculous not to feel inferior any longer, but a real person with her own place in life – above all, secure, loved and wanted.

Happiness must have gone to her head. She'd been over-confident, far too sure nothing could pierce the wall. She should have prevented Luke coming at any cost. It was then that the wall had begun to totter and crumble. There had been an invisible crack in it from the start – her relations with Luke, in which some disloyalty seems inherent, although she has never been disloyal in any way.

Throughout his visit she longed for him to be gone; and yet she still has this guilty feeling about him. At the same time, she detests him and his diabolical lemurs; between them they've destroyed her happiness as if by magic, and she is powerless against them.

The situation deteriorates rapidly from day to day. She and Chas quarrel, or else are silent, when they are together; which is not often, as he goes out more and more with people she doesn't know, leaving her alone. Every morning she wakes to a horrible hollow feeling, a gnawing pain that goes on till she next falls asleep, and is caused by the knowledge that she's in the process of losing him. Every night as she goes to bed she dreads waking up for another day.

And yet she does nothing . . . makes no effort to change . . . doesn't lift a finger to keep him. Now that the wall is in ruins, security gone, all confidence fatally undermined, she has relapsed into her childish sense of helpless inferiority. She's always alone, hardly speaks to a soul, nobody takes the slightest notice of her. It's almost as though she doesn't exist any longer. She feels she's only a kind of nothing ... a ghost who can't possibly alter the course of events or influence anyone ... nobody would listen to her.

Already she has almost forgotten the joy of loving and being loved. The memory of her happiness seems unreal, like a dream remembered from long ago. All that's left for her now is the horror of being alone and the pain of loss ... of being terrified, abandoned, betrayed ... the one person she has loved and trusted with all her heart transformed into a stranger, alien, untrustworthy, unkind.

*

Night is the worst time, when her vitality sinks to its lowest ebb and she's frightened of everything. Unable to read or do anything else, she wanders about the house like a woman living with ghosts, who can't find the way or the will to return to the living world. She stops by a window to see if there's a light in the studio (she knows very well there isn't), and pulls the curtain aside. Whereupon she forgets everything but what's in front of her eyes. Instead of the wintry darkness she is expecting, she sees the surrounding trees lit up as by a stupendous conflagration above. Vast corrugations of intense, pulsing, rainbow light move in slow, stately undulations over the northern sky, while spectacular serpentine streams of pure incandescence shoot across them, emitting a frigid unearthly brilliance. Sparkling with frost, the bare branches of the trees reflect the sky's blazing uncanny light, so that the whole wood seems on fire, burning resplendently with cold mineral flames.

She hurries out and stands on the frozen grass, staring up at the dazzle, absolutely astounded, until it dawns upon her that she must be witnessing a display of the northern lights. But that's impossible – the aurora borealis is never seen so far south. The staggering spectacle suddenly seems supernatural, terrifying ... and with a special significance for her personally, as if the illumination up there disguised a celestial messenger sent to warn her, as of the date of her execution, that the day for her to leave Chas is at hand. ...

This fatal message becomes an obsession, it's rarely out of her thoughts. Every day she feels herself more unreal ... destroyed without knowing how or why... swept along towards God knows what ghostly place of shadows... her happiness all a dream. Or perhaps she has never existed at all, and is simply an agonized shade in the mind of a dying person.

*

The man has ceased to recognize her as the carefree girl he was once so fond of. For a long time he has suspected her of a secret liaison with Luke, and her present melancholy neurotic attitude seems to confirm this, so that the last faint remnant of his affection expires and he detaches himself from her altogether. He can't bear to be in the house even, rushing away every morning, not coming back until after she has gone to bed.

She too often feels an urge to escape, and wanders aimlessly through the beech woods for hours on end. One day she finds herself in a small open space near the top of the hill from which their house can be seen far below, and her eyes fill with tears as she remembers how she used to think it looked from here like a friendly animal, waiting to welcome her back.

Now, although she's prepared for a change, its hostile aspect appals her. A premature twilight, a sort of blight, has suddenly come down on the afternoon, which was sunny when she set out. Looking up, she sees solid masses of great black storm-clouds racing across the sky, towards the one tiny patch of blue that's still left, symbolizing her doomed happiness, which is engulfed as she watches. Instinctively she lowers her eyes from the ominous clouds, just as their shadow covers the house, turning it into an evil black trap hidden among the trees purposely to catch her. A sudden cold wind makes her shiver... last year's leaves rustle and scurry along the ground.... All at once she is seized by a dread of winter, which seems to be lying in wait for her, only just out of sight.... Already she can feel its ice-cold breath on her face.

For a second reality fades, and, as in a dream, she sees a new ice-age approaching, great cliffs of ice flowing like lava over the face of the world... over mountains and seas and cities... men, fish, birds, animals, and machines that fly to the moon, all entombed together... preserved for ever in the ice of their common grave. She is petrified momentarily by this terrifying vision of doom, of polar ice advancing implacably to destroy all life.

But then the known world returns and she sees only what she

has seen so often: smooth column-like beech-trunks, some old tarnished ivy leaves on a bank. The foliage of the beeches is still thick enough to cast a black shade under the darkened sky. Every so often, a leaf silently flutters down like a stealthy threat of abandonment... isolation... a frightening reminder which makes her shiver again and clutch her coat tightly round her, overcome by her superstitious fear of winter's trap lying in wait – who will save her from it, now that Chas doesn't care any more?

Icy, sepulchral despair infiltrates the gloomy daylight. Alone in the midst of a frozen, enemy world, she is seized with the kind of panic a child feels when it first realizes the absence of familiar figures, and knows it is lost in a crowd.

On the point of crying and calling for help, in her despair, she suddenly feels something never felt before – a wild desire to be somewhere else, a desperate longing to escape from her present hopeless predicament, so strong that it almost amounts to a resolution to run away.

4

A SINGLE blast of the ship's siren had already warned visitors to go ashore; but very few of them had taken any notice of it, the great majority waiting for the two final blasts which, any minute now, would indicate that the actual sailing time had arrived. Meanwhile they stood about chattering, wandered aimlessly round the decks, or collected in groups, which obstructed free circulation and were a source of annoyance to the few people who had any definite purpose in moving about.

One of these, who'd been literally searching the ship, subjecting everyone to a close scrutiny, without ever catching sight of whomever he was looking for, now seemed to be losing hope. Sick of pushing his way through the crowd, he stopped on the fringe of a group collected around a professor holding forth on his coming tour, and stood leaning against the rail, still gazing, though with diminished expectancy, at the ever-shifting mass of strangers.

He'd got up very early to come here; his head was aching, and he was tired after his abortive search. His always rather gloomy face grew still gloomier. Irritable frustration sank to a lower depressive level now that he was no longer hurrying from deck to deck, going methodically through public rooms, knocking on cabin doors, darting in and out of unoccupied staterooms, thinking the whole time he must, must, *must* find her.... Well, he hadn't found her, and his chances of doing so were getting less every second. Probably she was not on the ship at all. He had no real reason to suppose she was ... except that he'd seen ... that he'd imagined.... Suddenly he felt a fool, trusting to a mere personal hunch and one or two vague clues, which now appeared like products of his imagination.

The question arose, as it did periodically in his mind, as to whether it was sensible, or even sane, to go on like this – dedicated to

finding someone who'd vanished utterly – living in a sort of submerged world consisting of endless journeys and endless streams of faces, none of them ever the right one. But he seemed to have no choice in the matter. It was as if he had been condemned....
He recalled an occasion – whether a long or short time ago he was unable to say, since his search already seemed to have lasted for an eternity – when, in some crowded station or custom-shed, he'd been startled by meeting the gaze of a pair of sharp greenish eyes which had seemed familiar, and had wondered if Chas could be searching too. A mass of bodies had at once intervened, separating them, so that he'd never been able to answer the question. But for some reason the problematic glimpse of the man who had been his friend had had the effect of rousing him momentarily from the curious uneasy sub-life to which he'd now reverted, restless as a fever dream, filled with incessant movement directed not by reason but by vague suspicions, guesses, omens and things half seen.

The cold wind brought a sudden gust of music, sweeping it away again before he'd recognized the tune. He knew the ship's band started playing only a few minutes before the time of departure. There seemed no point in staying on board till the last, and he decided to go ashore at once, thus avoiding the worst of the crowd.

He was moving away when a sudden screeching commotion made him look at some gulls squabbling over the ship's refuse, just as a much larger gull of a different kind swooped down on a special morsel, dispersing the rest in a flurry of flapping wings. Next moment the big bird sailed past him with barely a movement of its enormous wing-span, gliding up as if drawn at the end of an invisible string. He watched it rise over the boat-deck, which had been deserted when he inspected it earlier. Since then a solitary figure had appeared there, at which he stood staring incredulously – a girl whose extreme slenderness was not disguised by a thick grey hooded coat, rather like a schoolgirl's. Her back towards him, she seemed to be watching the people who'd disembarked and were standing on the quay, gesticulating and shouting incomprehensibly to friends on board. All at once his face changed and brightened, he eagerly hurried forward, convinced that she was the girl he'd been looking for everywhere. In spite of the distance between them and the fact that he hadn't seen her face, he was positive that he'd recognized her.

To reach the boat-deck he had to pass the group around the professor. Envying the big gull its effortless flight, he plunged in among all these people, who, determined not to miss a word now that time was so short, persistently obstructed him by pressing closer in a compact mass, so that he couldn't get through. He had made hardly any progress when the siren he was expecting and dreading sounded its two last fatal blasts with ear-splitting violence.

All those who were not sailing immediately surged towards the gangway *en masse*, sweeping him along with them. It was quite impossible to escape being caught up in this tide of determined humanity, which relentlessly bore him away from his objective and off the ship.

Once on the jetty, he saw the girl on the boat-deck again. She was now considerably further away and kept her head turned towards a woman who'd joined her, so that her face was still hidden. The doubts which had already invaded his mind increased as he watched the pair carrying on an animated conversation – surely this lively girl wasn't the one? He decided he must, after all, have been mistaken... but strange to say, he was quite unable to tell whether the discovery was a relief or a disappointment.

Suddenly the object of his attention turned, he saw her full face, and all his doubts disappeared in a flash, he forgot everything he had just been thinking, and once more felt certain of her identity.

She seemed to be looking straight down at him, and he waved enthusiastically, an involuntary smile, of which he was unaware, lightening his usually sombre features, while he pushed his way to the water's edge as if he intended to jump across the dividing gulf. His gesture, however, passed unnoticed amidst that forest of waving hands, and he let his arm drop, resuming his habitual pessimistic expression. Of course she hadn't been looking at him, but at the scene in general. Now she'd turned once more towards her companion, the hood partly hid her face, and he began to be doubtful all over again: but nevertheless he went on pressing towards the gangway, which was abruptly pulled up just before he reached it, as the steamer started to move very slowly away from the pier.

Luke looked appraisingly at the imperceptibly widening strip of water, which he could have jumped easily; noting at the same time that the position of the decks made this impracticable. The boat-deck was too high above him, its height increased by the rail; while the lower deck was equally inaccessible, being covered in, so that if he did jump across he would land on its roof. These calculations occupied him until the gap had broadened beyond any question of jumping it: whereupon he began shouting and waving his arms, endeavouring to attract the girl's attention, but without success.

The people he'd pushed aside were already glaring at him indignantly; and his shouts caused other more distant faces to turn towards him as if in astonishment. He was quite oblivious of them, entirely absorbed in the girl on board, still unable to make up his mind about her. One moment he was certain she was the girl he knew; the next just as sure she was not – the latter impression strengthened when she pointed at somebody in the crowd and burst out laughing – possibly at his own eccentric behaviour, for he was still trying to catch her eye by waving his arms like a semaphore. At last, noticing the annoyed or amused gaze of people near him, he abruptly ceased these antics: but still kept his eyes fixed on her receding and now indistinct figure, although common sense told him it was impossible to recognize anybody at such a distance, which moreover was increasing each moment.

The boat was now moving faster out into the harbour, its passengers united with those on land only by the flimsy paper streamers they threw one another. He himself, he discovered, was clutching one of the tight little paper rolls – how he'd acquired it was a mystery – which he hurled with all his might over the widening gap. He had an obscure notion that the unfurling ribbon was bound to reach her if she was the girl he wanted: and indeed it did actually get to the boat-deck, twining itself round the rail only a few inches from her – she could easily have picked it up without even moving. But, still chattering to her companion, she failed to observe its arrival.

The man on the quayside clenched his fists so violently that the semicircular imprints of his nails still marked his palms minutes later. But even now he didn't know what was causing him such intense anxiety – was he so urgently willing her to see the streamer, or not to see it? The boat had changed direction and was beginning to catch the full force of the wind, which blew a strand of hair across the girl's face, concealing it altogether. At the same moment his streamer was torn from the rail and whirled into mid-air, where it fluttered dementedly for an instant before falling into the chaos of tangled fluttering streamers below.

Stretched to their utmost, all the frail paper ribbons were breaking, hanging over the ship's side, floating for a second or two before they sank in the churning water. His spirits sank with them.

His thoughts began circling in endless claustrophobic spirals, which had all been there before and led nowhere. If he really loved Luz, surely he'd have taken some decisive action, instead of simply allowing her to disappear.... But of course he wasn't certain this girl *was* Luz. All the same, he surely wouldn't have risked losing her if.... He should have discovered her identity at all costs.... A terrible sense of finality accompanied the realization that she was lost to him irretrievably... the loss began to assume a monstrous significance.

'That was a splendid throw of yours – what a pity your friend didn't see.'

Frowning, he turned his head sharply. The speaker was a middle-aged woman he'd never seen in his life, wearing a long shapeless beaver-lamb coat like a disguise. She smiled at him amicably, full of generalized goodwill – she couldn't have chosen a more unresponsive recipient for it, or one to whom it was less welcome. He was so preoccupied that his politeness was quite in abeyance, and he merely said shortly, 'It's a futile custom in any case', relieved when she walked off without another word, doubtless taking offence at the rebuff.

Not aware of it, he stayed where he was, gazing sightlessly into the water at the bottom of the sea-wall which plunged straight down at his feet, reflected only as a fluctuating darker strip in the depths below. Even here in the harbour the water was too disturbed to act as a mirror, blown continually into small waves, its surface blurred by passing flurries of wind.

When next he looked up, the woman and most of the crowd had gone, while the ship was a good way out, executing the turn that would bring it round facing the open sea. Its decks were deserted now. Of a grey hooded coat there was no sign.

Nothing was to be gained by waiting any longer. But he couldn't bear to lose sight of this last, dubious, unsatisfactory link with the vanished girl, and went on standing there, watching the wide graceful curve of smooth water the ship left behind in turning, a calm pathway like the swathe of a scythe, over the turmoil created by its propellers, which had engulfed all the debris of sodden paper.

Little waves kept lapping the foot of the embankment, lifting the strands of fine seaweed, which seemed to come to instantaneous brief life, while they floated, glossy and green, only to be left limp and brown again on the stone. All at once a larger wave, perhaps caused by the ship's evolutions, perhaps by the rising tide, struck the wall with a loud slap, and he hastily stepped back from the spray. Looking round now, he had a puzzling sense of alteration in his surroundings. Not a soul was to be seen on the waterfront. He couldn't make out what had become of the huge metal gates through which he had entered, until he realized that an enormous crane had silently moved up behind him and was hiding them from view, though the men working it must have gone for their tea-break. When it occurred to him that these gates would probably be shut and locked soon, he at last turned his back on the harbour and started walking towards them.

He was quite near the crane when the cold wind carried a mournful hoot over the water, announcing that the boat was leaving the harbour's shelter and heading out to sea. He paused to look back at it. Already meeting the offshore waves, it looked absurdly small, a toy boat, intermittently disappearing behind the sullen grey masses of water charging along the skyline. To see it already at vanishing-point caused him a fresh pang. The whole world seemed to have become one great grey waste land, in which the fragile girlish figure had vanished without trace. Where should he start looking for her now? How would he ever find her again? If only he knew for certain whether she had, or had not, been the girl he'd seen on the deck. . . . Over and over again his tormenting thoughts revolved in the same futile groove, leading him in a circle. The only consolation he could find anywhere was in his old notion that the two of them were united by some obscure metaphysical bond . . . and even this seemed merely a bond between two dreamers, neither of whom could wake. . . .

In the course of these unhappy, fruitless meditations, his eyes had strayed away from the ship; and now, when he looked for it again, he wasn't sure he could see it – it could just as well have been any small smudge on the distant horizon. What was the use of looking after it, anyhow? That wouldn't bring it back . . . and, in any case, he wasn't certain. . . .

Sighing wearily, he walked on once more. All he could do was continue his interminable and hopeless search – wandering for ever all over the world, without any respite or real chance of success.

He felt tired, depressed, pessimistic, discouraged. Chilled through and through by the cold wind blowing down the back of his neck, he automatically turned up his coat collar and thrust his hands deep into his pockets as he strode along.

As soon as he'd passed the crane, he at once saw the towering gates standing open before him, each with a row of large black-backed gulls perched on the top of it, all facing into the wind, as motionless and identical as if they had been stuffed and put up there as a decoration.

5

IT was early morning and bitterly cold. Luz was on the deck of the car-ferry, leaning against the rail, taking no notice of the other passengers waiting to disembark. The landing-stage was quite near, a row of fir trees behind it standing out more distinctly than anything else in sight. Later there would be sun; but at this hour the sky was still overcast, a light mist hiding most of the landscape.

In the misty light the houses clustered at the end of the pier looked insubstantial, like houses of cloud, liable to change shape at any moment. She found their indefiniteness disturbing, and at once looked back at the trees. *They* were solid and gloomy enough, and so close now that they appeared to be presenting each separate black needle for her inspection.

In front of them, a few people had collected to await the ship's arrival. But from these she deliberately averted her eyes, not wanting to see any human being just then, apparently as oblivious of them as of the passengers crowding all round her. Divided by the rapidly narrowing strip of water, those on shore stared fixedly across at the people on board, the two groups confronting each other with oddly similar blank expressions.

Luz had successfully made herself unaware of both parties. And when presently a latecomer rushed up with a bag in each hand, almost bumping into her, she turned her head automatically but didn't really see him, immediately returning her gaze to the trees, at which she stared as though an exact description of them would be required from her at some future date. When the engines stopped, she was startled by the sudden silence, broken only by the thin cries of gulls and the swish of water against the sides of the boat, gliding forward under its own momentum.

*

Furious with the steward for forgetting to call him, the belated passenger had dressed in a violent hurry and rushed out on deck, grasping a bag in each hand: only to see that the crowd already waiting to go ashore was much too densely packed for him to insinuate himself among them and reach a favourable spot for disembarkation. He'd have to stand right at the back, and would probably be one of the last to get off the ship.

In his haste and exasperation he barely avoided colliding with the nearest person, a young woman in a thick grey coat with a hood rather like a schoolgirl's. It vaguely struck him as odd that, despite his preoccupation, he should notice what she was wearing, and even think that hooded coats seemed a winter uniform among women this year – he saw them everywhere, wherever he went. The wearer looked round then, giving him such a shock that all his ideas were thrown into wild confusion.

Luz herself seemed to have looked at him briefly, without recognition. He told himself that, of course, it couldn't possibly be Luz – Luz couldn't possibly not have known him. Nevertheless, the resemblance was extraordinary, so startling that he still felt staggered by it minutes later. He wished she'd look round again; but she never moved, leaning on the rail as if detached from what was going on around her, holding herself aloof from the crowd.

The likeness which had so astonished him left behind a curious residue of uneasiness. He couldn't help looking at the girl all the time: her stillness seemed disturbing and unnatural. And her position now struck him as strangely ambiguous, a contradictory mixture of resistance and resignation. If she'd been tied to the rail, she couldn't have kept more motionless, staring, like everyone else, at the land. Perhaps she was watching for friends or relatives who were to meet her; though he saw nobody who looked at all suitable, the group on the jetty consisting mainly of fishermen, idly gazing across at the passengers, who gazed back as if petrified, with identical blank faces.

The engines stopped. A collective movement of anticipation went through the waiting crowd; people picked up their hand luggage, or held their papers ready, with varying expressions of eagerness or anxiety. Only the girl looked as detached as ever, as though landing didn't concern her. She was still in the same posture, and the man found himself thinking how easily bonds could be concealed under the voluminous coat – a thought he instantly banished, since it belonged to an unacceptable part of his being which he was always trying to suppress out of existence.

A barrier was removed, people started to advance slowly, an open space appeared behind the backs of those just in front. He waited for the girl to step into it; then, as she did not do so, he went forward himself, glancing at her inquiringly as he passed. Although she seemed not to notice, he felt more uneasy, as though he should have told her the place was rightly hers. Yet, having taken it, he was reluctant to draw attention to what he had done.

*

She watched the gangway pushed out and seized by some of the men standing on the pier. Looking at them for the first time, she saw that they were all dressed alike, as if in uniform, but the uniform of a past era, its main item a full black belted tunic that seemed to be padded, which gave them a somewhat outlandish aspect, and did nothing to lessen the wholly unfavourable impression they made upon her. In all their faces she seemed to discern something fierce and frightening, much more alarming than the distrust of strangers common among peasants in remote localities. Thinking she wouldn't like to fall into their clutches, she looked away from them to the land.

The mist was gradually rising and breaking up, disclosing a wild scene of rugged, desolate beauty. The countless inlets, islands and jagged rocks of the coastline were backed by snow-capped mountains, their lower slopes covered in dense black fir forests like the close-clinging pelt of some wild animal. She tried to get excited, stimulated by the thought of landing in this strange northern country, so unlike the other countries she'd known; but succeeded only in feeling nervous and reluctant to do so. The nearer it came, the less she liked the idea of going ashore.

Although they were now more distinct, the houses still retained their unstable aspect, and looked curiously amorphous – some even seemed to be collapsing in ruins. Ghostly threads and tendrils of mist floated in the air, giving everything a hallucinatory appearance, which was intensified by the first evanescent glimmer of sunshine, come and gone again in a flash, like an illusion.

What was she doing here? Starting to feel odd and unreal herself under the influence of these deceptive appearances, she couldn't suppress her alarm at the prospect of visiting a place at once so indefinite and so intimidating.

*

The slow progress towards the gangway continued, depending on the length of time each person took to display his papers. Shuffling along with the rest, Luke still felt obscurely troubled and even looked back once or twice, half hoping to see the slight figure in the grey hooded coat advancing indignantly to claim his place. But she never moved, and standing alone there, apart from everyone else, had an abandoned air. Quite a long stretch of deck separated them now. Why he found her immobility so disturbing, he didn't know: but his uneasiness had become a definite anxiety on her account – he even considered going back and offering to see her safely ashore; which amazed him, as he hated talking to strangers.

At this point an interruption occurred in the slow procession. A man he'd already seen among the cars on the lower deck was now advancing like a strong swimmer against the tide of passengers moving the opposite way, pushing through them as if they weren't human beings but insentient objects obstructing him. Previously he'd noticed this individual only as the owner of a big black shiny Thunderbird, by far the grandest-looking car on board. Now he was disagreeably impressed, not only by the arrogant, inconsiderate way he was elbowing people aside, but by his whole appearance. Yet he supposed the pushing stranger would be considered handsome. . . . All of a sudden the haughty aquiline profile reminded him of a picture, seen long ago, of the pirates who had once sailed from here in their high-prowed ships to terrorize half of the world. That was it: the chap looked like a pirate and was behaving like one. As he thought this, he realized with dismay that the object of his criticism was making for the girl in the grey coat; in fact he called to her at this moment: 'What's the matter with you? Why are you still standing there? Have you gone to sleep?'

*

Lost in vague ruminations and staring towards the land, Luz had failed to observe the newcomer's approach. The sound of his voice gave her such a fright that she experienced a wild impuse to run back and hide in her cabin . . . jump overboard . . . anything to escape going ashore with him. . . .

She herself could not have said what it was about the man that affected her so strongly. A fierce, primitive sort of vitality radiated from him – from his compelling eyes and inscrutable countenance, from his silence and strangeness – powerful as a magician's wand, which had touched her and brought her helplessly under his spell. Since he monopolized her body and soul, it was most strange that at this moment she should have noticed, for the briefest fraction of time, another masculine face watching her in the crowd; a face which aroused a momentary flicker of hope by its familiarity, before it vanished, and she instantly forgot having seen it.

The onlooker was astonished to hear his own language spoken with barely a trace of an accent, and wondered if only the girl's reaction made him think the expressionless voice concealed the hint of a threat. She had swung round as if terrified out of her long immobility, not speaking a word. Even as far off as he was, he could see the hugely dilated pupils that made her eyes look black, blind and unfocused. Then, suddenly becoming conscious of the fixity of his own gaze, and that none of this was any business of his, he turned his back, occupying himself ostentatiously with his luggage. By an effort of will he banished the pair from his thoughts. But he looked round for them as soon as there was a hold-up, though it was obvious that they weren't in sight. His brain refused to accept this. He was still looking about for them when a bleak official voice drew his attention to the fact that he was the only passenger left on board. He was amazed to see that this was so; even those who'd been standing far from the gangway had disembarked and were already some distance along the jetty.

When he himself had walked about half its length he glanced round in case a grey hooded coat had appeared behind him; but no one at all was to be seen, either on the landing-stage or on the ship.

The ship . . . the ship where . . . the last place where. . . . He stopped abruptly. After being so struck by that astonishing resemblance, how could he have let the girl go without making sure of her identity? Back came his old painful uncertainties about his own feelings; to be violently rejected this time. All his doubts had suddenly vanished. Luz was the only human being he'd ever loved. An intolerable pain pierced him. He was totally lost without her . . . estranged from his life utterly, and from the world. This was the world into which he'd been born; the only world he would ever know. Yet nowhere in it did he feel in the slightest degree at home. *She* was his home . . . his one sanctuary upon earth . . . the only place of safety for him in the whole universe. But he had lost her . . . and consequently was condemned to absolute loneliness in an alien, frozen vacancy ... at the mercy of something huge, insensate and merciless as an eclipse.... For a moment his isolation was so agonizingly intense that it seemed impossible to go on living. He longed only to plunge into the black pit of annihilation opening before him.

Then a sudden sense of urgency seized him. There wasn't a second to lose. He must do something immediately....

He took a few hurried steps, then broke into a run. His mind in confusion, he was unaware of how his two suitcases impeded him, bumping into him with every step as he rushed on, obsessed by the necessity for speed, bounding over the lobster-pots and fishing-nets which littered the quay, at times coming dangerously near the unprotected edge. Too agitated to take any notice of obstacles, he might easily have come to grief on the slippery stones, some of which were covered in a slimy treacherous growth either of moss or seaweed. It was by sheer good luck that he escaped the various hazards and reached the end of the pier without any mishap.

Directly in front of him now were the grey indeterminate houses along the waterfront, a narrow street leading between them to an inner square, where he could see the station. Pausing to get his breath back, he heard a train whistle and afterwards travel rapidly out of earshot. Only a few scattered figures were moving about the streets, all wearing the regional dress, and not in the least like the passengers off the boat, who had all disappeared; they'd either gone into the houses or left by the departed train.

A feeling of helplessness and frustration had replaced his unbearable loneliness, and he stood without moving, not knowing what to do next. The only idea which occurred to him was to make inquiries at each house in turn, and this he at once discarded as futile. Of course these insular peasants wouldn't answer his questions. As a foreigner he'd automatically be suspect – regarded as a lunatic or a criminal; probably both.

He'd stopped beside a bookstall at the end of the pier, and the papers and periodicals in different languages spread out there gradually began to engage his attention. One of them, weighted down by four pebbles, was open at a picture headed 'Sea Rescue', showing an enormous black male arm clutching a fair girl against a background of stormy waves. The photograph seemed to have been taken by an amateur, as it was badly out of focus, the whole perspective so distorted that it seemed to record an act of violence instead of a rescue. The upper part of the girl's thin body was bent back so that her blonde hair hung down, mingling with the spray from the raging waters, into which the impossibly huge arm might have been thrusting her. The photograph seemed vaguely familiar, as if he'd already seen it somewhere... perhaps in the earlier editions he had read during the journey. Probably it was this very distortion that made him remember it....

Suddenly his expression changed, he forgot all about the picture, and looked round anxiously to see whether anyone was watching, overcome by embarrassment at the thought of his recent sprint. What an idiot, what an absolute bloody fool, he must have looked, leaping over lobster-pots as if in an obstacle race, and dashing along the pier with his bags. Anybody who'd seen him must have thought he was crazy, particularly if they'd noticed him standing here for the last few minutes, doing nothing whatever... just idling away the time at the bookstall... as if he was in no hurry at all and had all the time in the world... as if he'd never hurried in his life, and intended to waste the rest of the day idly staring at magazines....

Nobody, however, was anywhere near him. It was lunch-time and the streets were almost deserted. None of the few distant figures was looking his way. So, since the bookstall had been left unattended, he felt he could safely suppose that his temporary aberration had escaped notice.

6

DRIVING away from the ship, Luz could feel the silence of the village above the Thunderbird's low humming. By this time the sun had consumed the mist altogether. Yet the houses looked no more solid than they had from the boat, their outlines no more distinct. Many, she saw, really were collapsing in ruins, producing the queer amorphous effect she'd already noticed. The high-walled, narrow lanes seemed claustrophobic: and, in addition, she got an impression of emptiness, solitude, absence of life, in these winding, deserted alleyways, which was not adequately explained by the fact that most people were indoors, eating their midday meal.

Once a town of importance with its fortified harbour, this place of silence and toppling grey stones had now been reduced to a village, too big for its inhabitants, with only numerous massive abandoned structures to testify to the more prosperous, warlike past. Decay was ubiquitous; occupied buildings indistinguishable from ruins; cobbles merging without intervening pavements into heaps of rubble and subsiding walls. Instead of giving the walls definition, the bright light seemed to rob them of a dimension: nothing was stereoscopic. And the flat effect of a drawing seemed to her slightly disturbing in the thin, clear, heatless sunshine – frightening in its suggestion of unreality.

Nothing she saw was familiar enough to inspire comparison with other places she'd known; so that the idea of nothing here being real followed almost inevitably, and was confirmed by the house to which she was taken.

It was the last house, its imposing mass marked the village boundary, and was the centre of a group of more or less intact original buildings, which dwarfed the later dwellings to insignificance and stood out like a fortress against the pale blue sky. She'd been watching this impressive landmark for several minutes before the car turned into a short cul-de-sac terminating in front of it, where the cobbles widened into a sort of courtyard. This approach resembled a private road, all the neighbouring structures being derelict, the end house the only one to show signs of occupation. Built originally as an integral part of the great wall encircling the village, it still had the forbidding aspect of an armed fort. Looking at its blank façade, windowless but for a few slitlike apertures high up near the roof, she could scarcely believe such a place was lived in by present-day people. Yet when her companion told her it had been the home of his ancestors for hundreds of years, she at once saw how well it suited his lean, muscular, militant figure, his grim, good-looking marauder's face.

She had to make an effort to leave the car, which seemed an anachronism, blocking the narrow street. Reluctantly and with trepidation she passed through a huge ancient arched door, topped by armorial bearings, barred and ornamented with iron, heavy and massive enough for the door of a prison, the fortified walls looming far over her head. The interior, however, seemed – to a first glance, at least – reassuringly civilized, the sparsely furnished main rooms unexpectedly spacious and elegant, their polished floors reflecting the glimmer of dim old chandeliers.

Away from the street, the windows overlooked parklike stretches of grass, broken by groups of trees and jagged grey rock, sloping down to the fiord. Across and around the water, black fir forests gloomily climbed the first mountain slopes, spreading darkness throughout the scene, even in bright sunshine.

The slow striking of a clock somewhere reminded her that the ship they had come by stopped here only a very short time and must be due to leave. Simultaneously realizing that she was about to lose the last link with her past and with the known world, she opened a window and leaned out, hoping for a final glimpse of it. The boat had already gone. But although there was no sign of it, she still kept her eyes fixed on the fiord, which dominated the view in a rather oppressive fashion. No one looking out of any of these windows could possibly escape the sight of the grey-green water, blackish where it reflected black trees, curving away in the shape of a dragon's tail between wooded banks which occasionally rose into cliffs. There seemed to her to be something faintly menacing about the way it obtruded its motionless, mirrorlike, lakelike surface, which closed every vista, and looked as if frozen solid in its dead calm.

The tall handsome housekeeper who came to show her to her room seemed to take an instant dislike to her, judging by her icy, aloof manner. Without speaking a word, she strode ahead along dark winding corridors, turning at right angles again and again, never looking back to see if the girl was still following, until the latter was too bewildered to know whether they were in the same house or traversing labyrinthine adjoining ruins.

At last her intimidating escort paused momentarily at the foot of a steep narrow stair, rising into black shadow, informing her, still without turning her head, 'These are *your* stairs', putting a peculiar, mystifying emphasis on the personal pronoun. Up she went then, her tall black figure forbidding, her back, stiff and straight as a ramrod, radiating dislike, disapproval, and passed through a small lobby at the top before opening the door of the room beyond.

Luz was too breathless from hurrying after her to say more than thank you, so relieved by the woman's departure that she forgot to ask how she was to find her way down again.

Now the room claimed all her attention. It was like no other room she had ever occupied and struck her as very strange – its strangeness seeming far in excess of its unusual features. What most impressed her was the absolute silence, which was unnatural, no sound penetrating either from outside or from other rooms. Later on, when she discovered how completely it was cut off from the rest of the house, the narrow stairs leading nowhere else, so that whatever happened in it would be inaudible beyond its four walls, she understood why she had been given this particular room.

The few pieces of furniture were arranged in such a way as to leave the centre of the polished floor bare and empty, like a dance floor. A tremendously wide bed stood on a raised platform covered in sheepskin, and the soft, deep-textured skin combined with a warm-shaded lamp to produce a luxurious effect. The entire wall facing the bed was hidden by a gigantic mirror, more suited to a theatre than a house in a remote village. Confronted by her reflection here, she felt as though she were on the stage; and the theatrical suggestion might have been planned deliberately to augment her growing sense of being unreal.

*

Alone in the silent, isolated room, the only room to which the steep stairs give access, knowing no one can hear what takes place there – that no one is *meant* to hear – she feels totally vulnerable, at the mercy of the man with the pirate's face, who enters without knocking, without a word. Since she always sees him first in the mirror, he acquires the frightening unearthliness of the through-the-looking-glass-world: a mysterious, sinister stranger – how conceivably connected with her? – whose gloomy phantasmagoric arrogance is that of a pirate born out of time, defrauded of his bloodthirsty triumphs, yet convinced of his absolute right to despoil and ravish, overriding all opposition by his characteristic high-handed assurance, his inscrutable, haughty, contemptuous silence, his absolute determination to have his own way.

His eyes, always haunting the depths of the glass, icy grey-black like the fiord, are endowed with the destructive power of the deadliest weapons, piercing her eyes, penetrating her inmost self, and inflicting wounds through which her whole being drains into stupefaction... drowns in their frigid depths... while she is seized and taken as if under narcosis.

*

It is late at night, but the rose-shaded lamp by the bed is still on. Once again the words 'Have you gone to sleep?' are quietly spoken with a just perceptible accent by the voice that seems to hide an undefined threat beneath the absence of all expression.

The girl sits up abruptly but doesn't answer, watching the intruder implacably coming nearer to her through the glass with that slightly rolling gait pirates are supposed to have; and when he reaches the bed she bends her head, keeping her eyes lowered.

The man's hand finds its way under her chin, the extended finger and thumb stretching from ear to ear, and, pressing effortlessly on the jawline, forces her to raise her face. No matter how hard she tries to resist, she has to give way to the merciless pressure that tilts her face up, obliging her to meet his eyes, into which her eyes are drawn helplessly. She has the sensation of falling bodily into the bottomless abyss of his gaze... fixed on her with such persuasive mesmeric power that, as his hands fasten upon her shoulders and push her down, she sinks back obediently, and even makes small unconscious compliant movements shaping her body to his....

Later, he is sitting on the edge of the wide bed, still keeping a predatory hand on his prey, lying there at his mercy – so still as to seem dead. or entranced. Amidst the disarray of the bedclothes, his fingertips stray over her thighs, her stomach, her naked breasts; then trace the delicate outline of face and throat. Finally he slides his hand under her pale hair, again forcing her to lift her head and expose the large, darkly dilated, drugged eyes... into which he forces the inscrutable gaze of his own icy, impenetrable troll's eyes, then silently looks away. Withdrawing his hand, he lets her head fall back on the pillow, limp as a doll's, and without giving her another glance, leaves the room... where the soft click of the latch, the sigh of the closing door, his barely audible footsteps descending the stairs which lead nowhere else linger stealthily... threateningly... until silence once more reigns supreme.

An interval passes before the girl's reflection sits up in the mirror, her hair dishevelled, her expression blank, disorientated, lost and abnormal, like that of someone emerging slowly from deep hypnosis. Naked and shivering, she sits there in the middle of the big bed, now disordered as by a struggle, the coverings spilling over the edge of the platform and spreading along the floor.

The room is very cold, and her shivering grows more violent. But some more moments pass, as though there's a block in her brain – as if the message of cold has to reach her by some long, roundabout route – before she bends, stiff as a blonde clockwork doll, grabs the blankets, puts out the light and huddles down under the untidy covers, all in one automatic continuous movement. She has not uttered a word the whole time.

*

Her new unreal self is caught, imprisoned in the glass, where, no matter how hard she tries not to look, sooner or later she's bound to see it, frozen in poses of hypnotized acquiescence, a pale ghost with the mechanized motions of a walking doll, which eventually becomes indistinguishable from the real Luz.

As a foredoomed victim, she has had no alternative... her surrender seems preordained to this marauder armed with a sorcerer's powers, who all his life has taken whatever he wants without thought of payment. The moment he's attracted by anything, he has to have it... it's a sort of obsession, against which resistance is useless. In her case there has been none, he has advanced into territory subdued beforehand, encountering no opposition. Conquered without a struggle, she falls prone and helpless before him, as if she has been subject to him ever since time began. . . .

She even derives a certain relief from his savage embrace: his brutal love-making, depriving her of will – of her reality as a human being – reduces her to the status of his possession, and as such she feels more or less safe. Except when his cold, hard, statuesque face changes, sliding into an even more frightening murderous mask at moments of sudden rage . . . or when he withdraws into one of his terrible silences, lasting for hours, for days, leaving her entirely abandoned, utterly alone and forgotten.

On the far side of the looking-glass time is elastic and can't be measured. The bright, short, cold, northern days slip through her hands like beads. Winter has come very close to her and is still on her track. But although she knows winter must soon overtake her, unreality sets her fears at a distance . . . puts a remoteness between them.

A shadow herself among shadow actors, she plays her uncomprehended part in a foreign language . . . surrounded by devious looks . . . crooked smiles . . . half-heard alien voices whispering secrets.

7

OF course there was no hotel in the village. It was not the sort of place to attract visitors. Usually a room could be had at the café, but repairs were being done there at the moment, so even this accommodation was not available. The proprietor could provide only meals for the stranger, and suggest that he make use of a spare room in his sister's house, which was not far away.

The room turned out to be dark, depressing and devoid of conveniences. Its one concession to the twentieth century was an electric bulb dangling from the middle of the ceiling, where it lit neither the bed nor the table. In any case, the presence of an oil-lamp and a candle suggested that the supply of electricity was unreliable.

Little or no preparation, he noted, frowning, seemed to have been made to receive him. Numerous pieces of dark, heavy, old furniture crowded into the room without regard for appearances made it seem like a store-room, where someone had just made the bed and filled the big ewer with cold water. His frown, however, was automatic, part of his lifelong struggle to hide his isolation by imagining and then imitating the behaviour of other people in similar circumstances – he frowned merely because he believed displeasure would be the normal reaction, not because he himself was displeased by the room. Although he was used to a high standard of living within the framework of civilization, by far the greater part of his life was spent in solitary travel in remote places, and under conditions far worse than these. Without investigating the thought, he vaguely supposed that his present surroundings were 'suitable'. And it was true that the room matched his gloomy, severe expression; though this almost certainly was not what he meant.

His two suitcases, one on top of the other, occupied the only space previously left vacant by the furniture, directly in front of the window, where he stood looking out at the remains of an ancient protective wall, which had encircled the village in the old days. Now half in ruins, its upper part had collapsed in a cascade of rubble on to open ground sloping down to the fiord. The yard that must once have divided the house from the wall no longer existed, this area too being full of the debris nobody had bothered to clear away, piled up nearly to the height of the window.

There was a knock at the door. The frown still on his face, he called out 'Come in!' and an elderly, poorly dressed woman entered.

'Here's the key.' Stopped, probably, by his frowning face, she remained just inside the door, without relinquishing the big heavy key in her hand, surveying him with an expression no more amiable than his own, until she finally said: 'You won't forget to lock up after you, will you?'

As he'd already given an assurance on this point when asking for the key so that he needn't disturb her if he came in late from the café, he replied irritably that she need not worry – hadn't he told her he would see to it?

She said nothing, but still went on standing there, watching him suspiciously, twisting the key in her gnarled fingers with their enlarged joints, as if she couldn't bear to part with it; and he realized that she was regretting having agreed to let him the room when her brother had urged her to do so for the sake of the money. Probably she was afraid of having a strange man, and a foreigner into the bargain, in the house where she lived alone; perhaps wondering whether he was a criminal who would murder her in her bed.... With an effort, he again recited the story concocted on the spur of the moment: that he was a perfectly respectable traveller who merely wanted a quiet room in which to work undisturbed on the book he was writing about his journeys. But the repetition appeared to have no effect. She continued to look at him so distrustfully that he saw she might really decide to throw him out even now, in spite of her obvious poverty – a serious matter, since there seemed to be no alternative accommodation – and that he must somehow persuade her to let him stay.

In exasperated silence, he produced his notecase, extracted several notes and laid them on the top of the suitcase in front of him – the money would talk more convincingly than he could. The amount was ridiculously excessive for such a poor, comfortless room, and it occurred to him, too late, that his eagerness to take it as demonstrated by this lavish overpayment, might only increase her suspicions. It would have been quite enough to display the sum she had asked for, which indeed was already much more than the room was worth.

To his relief, however, avarice apparently overcame her fears at the sight of such wealth, and she handed over the key, snatching up the notes immediately afterwards as if afraid he might change his mind.

*

As soon as the visitor came in after lunch, he went straight to the window and stared out so intently that he seemed to be looking for someone, although as usual there was no sign of life out there; nothing moved.

The scene had a rugged, sombre impressiveness, but was gloomy in the extreme, composed entirely of shadings of black and grey, which awaited only the imminent stark white of snow to add the finishing touch to its desolation. His eyes fixed themselves on the fiord which was its centre – anybody who didn't know would take it for a lake, it was so motionless, the slow ebb and swell of the tides perceptible only during exceptionally stormy weather. No other houses were visible from here, this one being on the very edge of the village. Even the remains of the massive wall soon collapsed altogether, leaving just the bare sloping ground, now covered in dead vegetation. At the foot of the slope, the glassy water, exactly reflecting black trees, looked lifeless, funereal, in its dead calm, emitting a pallid and ghostly gleam. Something malignant seemed to be rising from it – suddenly it appeared to him as the source of the surrounding gloom. No wonder the local people believed it was bottomless and the home of some kind of monster.... Before his eyes, the forest was taking on a threatening impenetrable aspect, the whole wild mountainous landscape assuming an air of ferocity it derived from the fiord... from something savage and prehistoric which dwelt in its unplumbed depths... something always hungry for victims... perpetually demanding a living sacrifice....

These last thoughts were just below conscious level, and, as if to avoid recognizing them, he moved away, taking several turns up and down the restricted space, before he seemed drawn back to the window.

Immediately then he leaned forward, staring out with a fresh interest. Although he couldn't see it, he knew that a narrow path skirted the fiord, running on into the forest, and he seemed to have caught sight of a woman down there, just before she vanished among the trees. His impulse to rush off in pursuit was checked by considerable doubt as to whether he'd really seen anyone, since he'd had the same impression before and followed it up, without ever finding the person he'd hurried after, or anybody at all. Nevertheless, he turned to pick up his coat, still lying on the bed where he'd thrown it a few minutes earlier; but, having done so, stood in uncertainty, holding it in his hands. His hesitation was mainly due to the idea that the figure he seemed to have seen was a kind of delusion; but now the landlady was involved as well. He was sure she kept a close watch on his movements, and she would undoubtedly feel inquisitive as to why he was going out again now, just after he had returned from the café.

Oh, to hell with that! Suddenly furious with himself, he thrust his arms violently into the sleeves of his coat, his decision made for him. This was one of the times when the importance he attached to the opinions of others enraged him; when he felt only abysmal contempt of the diffidence and desire for conformity thus implied.

Eager to show his independence, he went to the door; but instantly hurried back to the window, opened it, and stepped easily from the sill on to the heaped rubble outside, pulling the window shut after him with the tips of his fingers, before climbing over the wreckage. With conflicting feelings, he strode rapidly down the slope, elated at having hit on this method of evading his landlady's supervision, but also astonished and rather embarrassed by his own eccentric act, which seemed most out of keeping with his usual behaviour.

*

He always avoided the village, which struck him as being entombed in its violent past like Lot's wife in her pillar of salt: its inhabitants seemed more behind the times than many primitive tribes, fixed as they were on a lost warlike supremacy, even their clothes based on obsolete military uniform. Apparently the present day meant less to them than their former world-invading expeditions of conquest, rape and rapine, of which they must have been constantly reminded by the derelict fortifications they lived among. The consistently hostile attitude they'd adopted towards himself was only to be expected, and suited him very well. He was glad that, even now after he'd been coming to the café for some days, no one ever spoke to him there except the proprietor, and he only in a professional capacity.

His long, solitary, daily walks were always in the direction of greater loneliness, into the sombre, mountainous country that appeared to stretch on and on endlessly, and to be totally uninhabited. Not once in the course of his wanderings had he encountered a single soul. Nothing could have astounded him more than to hear, returning at twilight one evening, several voices speaking together quite near him, although nobody was in sight.

Its feeble lights coming on one by one like a dim cluster of glow-worms, the village was still some distance away, and he was certain there were no houses nearer. Having stared all round without discovering where the voices came from, he turned to the fiord. But there was no sign of a boat on the flat expanse of water, which looked solid enough to walk on, like a sheet of glass or dark ice. In that lonely stillness, and in the fading light, the apparently disembodied voices sounded unearthly. The uncanny effect was increased by a number of vast, rounded boulders, torn from the mountainside in some prehistoric upheaval, which lay together at the water's edge, looking like severed heads after a mass execution of giants. Each was as big as a cottage, and all appeared much the same shape in the dimness. Only when a lamp showed yellow against the blue dusk did he realize that one of them was the work of man, and the place where the speakers had congregated.

Suddenly curious about such an improbable gathering in this wild, remote spot, he left the path and approached the lighted window, stopping before he was close enough to be seen from inside. His footsteps were soundless on the thick grass. In any case, the others were making far too much noise to have heard them.

The small, low-ceilinged room was crowded; there was much smoke, many raised voices talking at once. At first he was too confused and dazzled to make anything of the disconnected scraps of talk that were audible, or to recognize the various gestures, limbs, faces, swimming in the haze as in a tank full of smoke and uproar. So many outlandish figures in their archaic dress, all packed tightly into this small space, their faces red as if reflecting flames, thick smoke swirling all about them, reminded him of some primitive picture of hell.

The first person he recognized definitely was an elderly man described by the café proprietor as a leading figure, employed, as most of them were, by the owner of the last house in the village, who seemed to stand in a sort of feudal relationship to its inhabitants. The old fellow's daughter, housekeeper at that same house, was the one woman present in the room crowded with men. The onlooker recalled the proprietor's words to the effect that she was 'worth any two men in the district', which could have been more than a manner of speaking, for the handsome, forbidding female was nearly as tall as her father, and had the same stern, resolute, unrelenting expression.

The old man seemed to be telling a story, though few people could have heard what he said. His voice went on steadily as if relating something he knew by heart, the actual words mainly inaudible. From the few phrases that reached him, the listener gathered that he was recounting an old local legend which must have been familiar to all those present: every winter, a beautiful young girl had to be thrown into the fiord from the high rocks to appease the dragon that lived in its lowest depths. Swirling up to the surface, the hideous monster, which had a snake's body and doglike head armed with long pointed teeth, tore the living victim to pieces before the eyes of those making the sacrifice.

Some connection between the present gathering and the story had prompted the telling of it. But this the man outside could not follow, although the noise had slowly begun to subside. Hearing a reference to rumours from further north, followed by something unintelligible about ice melting or moving, he recalled snatches of talk he had caught at the café, in which these same rumours had been mentioned, but he remained as much in the dark as ever.

Silence fell by degrees. People stopped talking among themselves to listen to the narrator, who was now giving details of the actual ceremony, speaking all the time in the present tense and as if he himself habitually took part in the sacrifice. 'We tie her hands, but not very tightly, and leave her feet free so that she can struggle a bit. If the dragon didn't see her struggling he might think we'd palmed off a dead girl on him.... As soon as she's kneeling at the edge of the rock, the water below starts boiling ... we can see the

dragon's great scaly coils.... We hurl her down, and the whole fiord becomes a maelstrom, blood and foam fly in all directions....'
The last words were uttered with dramatic satisfaction into dead silence: but immediately afterwards a perfect babel of voices broke out, everyone again talking at the same time, so that the listener caught only unrelated fragments of what was said.

To his surprise, all the dour, glum faces had suddenly become eager and animated; and from this fact, rather than from anything he could hear, he concluded that they were discussing the sacrifice with the same gusto and personal interest they would have displayed over a football match between their own and a rival village. It was, obviously, a topic with which everyone in the room felt passionately concerned, and in no mere theoretical way either.

'There aren't so many good-looking girls as all that – why should the dragon get the pick of the bunch?'

This new loud facetious voice spoke just inside the window, every word came clearly through the pane, causing a lot of laughter and exclamations.

'And why should we sacrifice one of our girls, anyhow,' it went on, 'when an outsider would do just as well? Some girl who isn't connected with us....' The meaningful tone of the assertive voice conveyed the idea that the speaker had a particular individual in mind, and that the others would know who was meant – evidently they did, for this new suggestion started heated arguments all over the room.

The meeting divided itself finally into two opposing groups: the elders, who wouldn't hear of any change in the established ritual, and the younger men, determined not to lose an attractive girl.

'You can't play tricks on the dragon!' The angry voice of the old man who'd related the legend drowned the rest. 'The dragon's been starved far too long already....'

Now an extraordinary interruption occurred: his daughter, who'd said nothing so far and was busy across the room filling the mugs and glasses extended by massive hands, looked up suddenly and shouted at him, though she was too far off for her voice to be heard through the window. The onlooker just had time to see the outraged expression on the old man's face before he swung round to answer, so that his words were lost too.

Putting down the jug she was holding, the housekeeper pushed through the crowd of men and confronted her father with arms folded and flashing eyes, apparently challenging him. She looked so intense and intimidating that the watcher instinctively took a step back, again missing what was said. So far he hadn't heard a word and had no idea why they were arguing, but, approaching again, he was amazed by the distortion of the woman's mouth – she seemed to spit the furious words at her father, whose face was on a level with her own.

'I tell you, it's got to be done!'

She was almost screaming, shouting at the top of her voice, so that every word was distinct as she launched out into a venomous tirade against 'pale, thin girls who looked as pure and angelic as if they were made of glass.... I'd like to smash them all to smithereens!' was her furious conclusion. 'I'll hurl her down off the rock myself, if none of you have the guts to do it!'

Breathless, her chest heaving, she turned her head to gaze all round the room, her blazing eyes shooting invisible rays of scorn at the men, who shifted uneasily or muttered among themselves, taken aback by her viciousness. The father lifted his clenched fist as if meaning to strike her down; but she was quite undaunted by his threatening pose, again standing face to face with him, drawn up to her full height, her expression contemptuous and utterly without fear.

A hush had fallen upon the villagers, who were all watching with round, avid eyes – such a public scene between two of their leading personalities must have had immense drama – when, before the raised fist had time to descend, a new voice that had not been heard broke the charged silence with a seriousness and urgency which immediately diverted the general attention and relegated the quarrel to unimportance.

'Stick to the point! Stop wasting time over side issues! We've got to act, and act quickly.... Don't you realize there's hardly any time left? My brother who's come down from Nordkaap used to hear the glaciers roaring closer each night!'

The words raised a storm of voices in the small room. But, at this point, the listener out in the dark turned abruptly and walked away from the cottage as fast as he could. These peasants were worse than savages, he was thinking, noticing at the same time that he was half frozen – it served him right for standing there all that time listening to such a ridiculous rigmarole. Since when had he become so interested in village gossip? Angry with himself for indulging in this grotesque eavesdropping, he walked back to his lodgings as fast as was possible in the darkness.

As soon as he'd taken his coat off indoors, he got out the notebook in which, to pass the time as much as to confirm the reason he'd given for wanting the room, he'd begun writing down all he remembered about a certain tropical island, the one place in the world inhabited by a race of mysterious singing lemurs known as the Indris. He had a curious, deep, almost mystical feeling for these rare, gentle, tree-dwelling creatures and their weird, fascinating songs, and in thinking about them quickly forgot the barbarous talk he'd been hearing.

He had just described his long search for the Indris, struggling for days through dense jungle without finding a trace of their presence, until he'd begun to wonder if they had any existence except in local legend and imagination. The whole subject was of intense interest to him, occupying his mind so frequently that he wrote without effort, the sentences seeming to form of their own accord.

Now, however, he paused and sat motionless, pen in hand, gazing at nothing. He had reached a climax of his narrative and was recalling the wonderful day when, just before sunrise, from the trees all round him, had burst a pure, sweet, melodious chiming, as of hundreds of golden bells – the overture to the unearthly music he was about to hear for the first time. Even then he hadn't managed to see the lemurs; and they still remained invisible when they repeated their strange concert at sunset. This state of affairs went on for several days longer, the shy singers always keeping out of sight, hidden in the tops of the great trees, where they conducted their secret life screened by the many layers of leaves, moving swiftly and silently through the branches, while he blundered after them on the ground, hacking his way through the undergrowth, with only their morning and evening chorus to guide him.

This period he regarded in his own mind as a time when, in some obscure way, he'd been put on trial and eventually not found wanting. Yet he'd never understood why the Indris had at last decided to trust him, accepting him as harmless and even friendly ... appearing before him quite openly from then on, allowing him to fondle them and play with the young ones....

Instead of writing all this down, he went on sitting in a sort of waking dream, brooding vaguely over the music which had haunted and held him enthralled ever since that original hearing. The peculiar spell the singing exerted over him was so potent that he gradually seemed to be hearing a faint echo of it in the midst of his ruminations ... a sound which by degrees grew louder and more compelling, until it filled his head, inducing an almost entranced condition.

8

THE room with its own staircase lost none of its strangeness for the girl who occupied it without ever feeling at all at home there. Yet she often retreated to it, the one place she could call her own in the vast, rambling, fortress-dwelling; the one room where she was not apt to be suddenly startled by the silent approach of the formidable housekeeper. The woman intimidated her more and more as time passed. On some days she actually seemed to pursue her with spiteful looks and comments, as though driven by a compulsive urge to vent her unremitting antagonism, incomprehensible to its object, who was too innocent, or too preoccupied, to guess its probable reason.

Now she was trying to concentrate on a book and ignore her surroundings; but her attention kept wandering towards a suppressed idea she refused to acknowledge ... until it began to come between her and the printed page ... forcing her to realize how her eyes were continually being drawn to the great mirror by an attraction that threatened to become irresistible at any moment.... Whereupon she jumped up, quickly put on her heavy coat, and, feeling unpleasantly nervous, hurried along dark twisting corridors which were now familiar, and left the building.

The air outside was so cold that it took her breath away for a second. But the sun was shining brightly – which she hadn't noticed indoors, as the small, deeply recessed windows were difficult to see out of – and was sparkling on the white slopes of grass in front of the house, where each separate blade was now stiffened with rime.

Glittering with frost, the wild, sombre landscape looked less forbidding, only the trees still radiating their usual gloom. The sinister black forest spread everywhere, it was impossible to avoid it. However, she took a path she knew well by the water, which dipped only briefly into the trees, soon coming back into the open.

The cold intensified as the narrow track entered the forest, where black tangled branches made almost a solid roof, penetrated only by a spattering of gold sunspots. The chaotic masses of trees shut out the view entirely, showing nothing but an occasional glint of water. Suddenly she looked for the fiord, failed to find it, and instantly felt uneasy. It seemed a long time since she'd last seen it – why was she taking so long, much longer than usual, to get out of the trees?

Anxiety quickened her steps. But it was impossible to hurry in the forest. Immediately an unseen root tripped her, so that she almost fell... a branch, simultaneously tugging her back, caught in her hair, lashing out at her viciously when it was disentangled. The trees seemed to obstruct her intentionally, with deliberate malice....

Trying not to see how alarmingly they were closing in, she stared round intently for the fiord, without which she couldn't even tell whether she was walking the right way. But nothing was visible except the black tent of the forest; and seeing that it was no longer pierced by gold pinpoints of sunshine, she was at once seized by a new fear, thinking the sun might have set already, overcome by a childish terror of these black trees surrounding her, horrifyingly tall, their utter stillness suggesting concentrated attention. If only something would move and attract their attention from herself. But she alone moved. Everything else was frozen, immobile. The whole forest had frozen in watchful attentiveness, far too full of its uncanny, malevolent life, which was draining away her own. She was growing less real every second... more spectral... a ghost-woman, imprisoned by black walls of towering trees on all sides... caught by the forest as in a monstrous trap.

It all seemed to have happened to her before. She seemed to know this terror darkening the air. The past, that was where it came from, the fear she felt now... this sensation of weakness and unreality in all her being... these shivers running down her spine. She'd already experienced them, and now they'd again overtaken her. The anguish, the terror, the derealization, were part of a repetitive pattern... the pattern of the victim, swept along helplessly to her destruction, doomed without knowing why.

Just as she was sinking in total despair, the steely cold gleam of water appeared through the dark mesh of branches. But her relief was only momentary. She was not really reassured, even when she finally extricated herself from the trees. Unnerved by the savage, desolate landscape, she felt the primitive dread of something alert but invisible, watching her, waiting to pounce; and this superstitious fear made it only too clear that she had escaped nothing by running away.

She was afraid to look up, but now nervously forced herself to raise her eyes to the mountain slopes, bristling with trees like guns, in stark black outline against a lurid red sky. So the sun really *had* set. And she must be miles from the village. She'd never get back in daylight.

For a moment she stood petrified, while the absolute silence and loneliness of the scene grew quite horrifying, hiding unspeakable terrors, and the immutable seemed poised on the edge of change, no longer static, the atmosphere turning fluid. Under the spell of the approaching night, everything was starting to slide into nightmare before her eyes . . . the mountains an impassable fortified wall, beneath which the massed trees assumed the menacing solidity of an encamped enemy army, and closer crouching clumps of bushes disguised the lairs of unimaginable monsters.

Invaded by sudden panic, she began running towards the fiord, which had taken on the incredible look of an icy volcanic crater about to erupt, its black waters enclosing a baleful, incandescent heart, which was the reflected sky. Ghostly tentacles of steam or mist were rising all over the surface, one of these spectral shapes gliding straight towards her. It was already almost upon her before she saw it . . . and stopped, with a stifled cry, arrested by its clammy touch, enveloping her in a chill, ectoplasmic substance, resisting her most desperate efforts to throw it off until, in its own time, it withdrew, pursuing a swift, erratic course, flitting furtively about the landscape, occasionally intertwining with other similar pallid ghosts.

At once she ran on, not daring to leave the water, her only guide, but averting her eyes, afraid of what might emerge next in this livid half-light, where any horror was to be expected. Pools had accumulated among the dead reeds, over which she jumped wildly, but often not far enough, so that she shattered the ice, sending up fountains of spray, barely conscious of the freezing shower-bath, or of anything but the appalling sound of another runner's feet thudding just behind her. She was too exhausted to recognize the thumping of her own heart, until, just as it seemed about to burst through the walls of her chest, she saw the scattered lights of the village in front of her.

Panting, hardly able to stand, she leaned again a tree-trunk, taking great gasping gulps of cold air more like sobs of relief. But when, as soon as she'd recovered slightly, she hurried on again, she was aware of a different sort of anxiety – fear of being seen by the housekeeper, her implacable enemy, who was sure to make cutting remarks about her dishevelled state and might even pass on a distorted account of it to her employer. At the same time, she felt ashamed of her own inability to stand up to the woman, who was only a subordinate, yet she knew she'd never be able to, seeing herself indistinctly as the victim and target of all ill-feeling, who must accept every wound and indignity.

In the hope of avoiding a meeting, she was making for a side door that was little used and generally left unlocked during the day. The last faint pallor of twilight was still in the sky, against which the threatening medieval mass stood out pitch-black with its towers, turrets and battlements which wouldn't have withstood modern weapons for half a second, yet looked as grimly indestructible as the jagged peaks of the mountains behind. Groups of firs buttressed the place with the extra blackness of their shadow, through which she advanced cautiously over a carpet of frozen needles.

No light was showing inside, and, as she'd hoped, the door had not yet been fastened. But, although she was wet through and shaking with cold, she hesitated, inexplicably unwilling to enter.

*

All of a sudden, she remembers her lost happiness. For an infinitesimal fraction of time she again experiences that almost forgotten sense of security and belonging... the bliss of loving and being loved, transforming life into supreme happiness, such intense joy that the surrounding air vibrates and sparkles with gaiety. In a flash it's all over. She's back in her aloneness. No vibration, no sparkle, no happiness. Gaiety is unthinkable. Happiness is dead, finished, nothing... perhaps it never existed.

She is left with a vague impression that the illusion has visited her for some urgent reason which she fails to recognize. And when she finally makes the effort of going through the door, it's as if the old inescapable forces of destiny are inside, awaiting an appointment with her made long ago. Once more the thought that she's escaped nothing by coming here goes through her head. But now remoteness has settled on her again, putting everything at a distance. Her whole life here in this fortress seems quite fantastic, unreal. She even distrusts the reality of what is before her eyes, confronting an open door into a dim hallway with a staircase she's never seen before. A life-sized Apollo stands at the foot of the stairs, upholding a lamp, or perhaps a lyre: and where the other newel post ought to be, a stern-faced, winged Mercury, poised for flight, seems to be staring straight at her, as if she's to be the recipient of his baleful message.

Of the housekeeper there's no sign. The whole huge cavernous building is silent and seems deserted, as, her hands stretched out in front of her, she feels her way along the walls of the dark corridors, afraid a light will draw attention to her arrival. Without meeting anybody at all, she slips into her lonely room, quietly shutting the door. She's safe from the housekeeper now, but has no sense of having reached security. The room is coldly unfriendly, its atmosphere alien, strange as always. Its walls withhold their protection from her. The book, lying forlornly where she has dropped it, gives the effect of a room from which people have fled in terror.

*

Tonight she has gone up to bed early, feeling more comfortable than usual in her peculiar room because the pirate-faced man is not in the house. Of course his absence is only temporary. He will be back tomorrow. But for tonight at least she need fear no intrusion. With an agreeable sense of relief and freedom, she curls up on the bed in her dressing-gown, and reaches out for a book on the table under the lamp.

The movement draws her eyes to the mirror, where her reflected arms resemble the stalks of two etiolated plants, reaching out to the light. The sight of that hallucinatory through-the-looking-glass world, where she sees herself floating in space, at once abolishes her relaxed mood. She forgets the book, her customary uneasiness returning, and vaguely watches the two pallid arms uncertainly wavering in the glass, reminding her of strands of pale weed under water.

Suddenly her heart gives a tremendous leap, and goes on beating rapidly and erratically, as, in the mirror, she sees the door slowly opening. To her amazement, this time it's the housekeeper who comes in, with no preliminary knock, her black figure menacing and tall as a tree, and standing silently just inside the room.

A wave of acute apprehension overwhelms the girl on the bed, who suddenly knows that something frightful is about to take place . . . something that's been coming to her from the very beginning. It's no mere accident that has left her unprotected tonight. All at once everything appears prearranged. The end of this scene has been planned in advance long ago, rehearsed many times in secret, and now nothing can stop its being played out to the appointed end. Just as nothing can stop the expression of terror she feels congealing upon her face, as she slowly turns from the glass to look directly at the dread, motionless form at the door, and sees, straight away, the expected glint of merciless triumph in the hooded eyes. At the same time she dimly discerns another tall shape, masculine but unidentifiable, standing in blackest shadow.

'What do you want?' She brings out the whispered words with the utmost difficulty, scarcely able to speak at all, or even to breathe, her heart is racing so wildly.

There's no reply: only the basilisk stare fixed upon her, increasing her sense of foreboding. Nobody says a word. The silence swells to horrific proportions, enormous, filling the room. And yet the profound stillness of the lonely room seems only a premonition of some even deeper silence awaiting her . . . a still greater isolation.

The tableau has crystallized in the mirror, where the reflected girl stares back as if mesmerized, out of eyes so widely dilated that they look black, like two deep pits of terror. While the girl on the bed, hands agonizingly clasped on her breast, so exactly resembles her double that there's no possible doubt they are one and the same. Her eyes too are hugely black with dread of the fate she already half knows by intuitive nightmare foreknowledge.

They all remain suspended or as if turned to stone, until at length the forbidding woman commands 'Come here!' in a harsh, peremptory voice, the two syllables crashing like stones into the glassy hush . . . which does not break, but simply absorbs them, as it absorbs the tranced motions of the girl, who obediently steps down and approaches the speaker, whose emanations of vicious hatred it absorbs too, along with the forward move of the shadowy form in the background.

The two tall, powerful figures, elderly man and woman in the prime of life, grab the arms of the victim and tower over her as over a slight, terrified, helpless child, whose feeble cries and struggles they suppress instantly.

The room watches this climax with satisfaction. It has won. It has been inimical to the end, and is now ejecting the intruder for ever. She far removed in her victim's trance, in a dim, instantaneous flashback, returns with her mind to a different existence, another world, millions of years away ... and a pellet of mangled and bloody flesh, the pill of food regurgitated by an owl, which small compressed bolus of crushed flesh and bone and internal secretion she has now become.

9

THE song of the Indris, lingering in the man's head, changes to a sound between a wail and a howl, then expires abruptly, while at the same time all thoughts connected with them are completely erased from his mind.

A full moon shines overhead, small, cold and exceedingly bright, high up in a sky flashing with big frosty stars. Tall, perpendicular rocks support the flat horizontal rock, powdered with frozen snow, on which he is standing. It might be a high-diving platform, except that its projecting ends dimly suggest rudimentary arms – in fact, the whole strange rocky formation faintly resembles a crude, incomplete, primitive monument, and seems vaguely familiar to him. Yet he is sure he has never been here before, where stark towering cliffs rise straight up out of the fiord, the edges of which are frozen, he observes from his lofty position, although further out, at the foot of the promontory, black, mirror-bright water is reduplicating the moon.

This doubled moonlight reveals everything very clearly. He has already recognized the frail, shuddering, naked girl, huddled at the end of the platform just in front of him, on whom all his attention is fixed. The whispers and restless fidgeting of a crowd of people behind him scarcely impinge on his notice; he isn't interested, and doesn't even look round, never taking his eyes off the helpless figure ahead.

Her hands are tied loosely behind her back. But at some period she must have struggled against her bounds, for, with a sudden surge of the old detested excitement, he sees how deeply the cords have cut into the tender flesh of both wrists. Her struggles have now ceased. Cold, exhaustion and terror have reduced her almost to the point of collapse. Her legs, bent under her, seem to have given way; which does not detract from the grace of the thin white body so near him ... under his eyes ... within reach of his hand.

Impulsively, one hand moves forward, but he checks the gesture at once. . . . His eyes are fastened on the delicate wrists, no thicker than the bone he believes he could snap with his bare hands. A familiar, hideous thrill runs over his nerves . . . an overwhelming sensation, far beyond control . . . a sort of illicit, unholy joy. He wants to watch her suffer, to see her bleed. . . .

The end comes far too quickly for him. The old fellow who related the legend at the cottage meeting approaches with two burly fishermen, forcing him to draw back slightly. But the moonlight is so strong that he can still see distinctly the huge, darkly dilated eyes of horror the victim turns to her executioners. Finding no pity on their faces – or on his either, for that matter – a pathetic childish grimace contorts her face . . . big tears spring from her eyes, which the moon transforms into diamonds as they roll down her cheeks without a sound. Her bound hands twitch ineffectually once or twice, like wounded birds, in an instinctive, hopeless attempt to free themselves.

The unseen crowd is growing impatient; there is a muttering and a stamping of feet on the iron-hard ground. Without further delay, the three men seize the weeping girl, who looks like a child compared with their muscular massive maleness, and hurl her over the end of the rock. White as a falling star, she plummets down in the moonlight, her bright hair streaming behind like a comet's tail. Her thin last piteous scream is drowned by the ensuing splash, and, with a hateful, ecstatic sensation, the onlooker sees the black water spurt up and wash over her in a flood, filling her eyes and throat and tearing her limbs apart, possessing her fully, as he never has done.

The whole fiord immediately becomes convulsed. The ice breaks up with cracks loud as pistol-shots. The threshing tail of the monster sends great waves dashing against the upstanding rocks, bursting in wild cascades of spray. Oblivious of the freezing drops showered upon him, the watcher sees the slimy, repulsive coils of the dragon protrude obscenely, like swollen intestines, from the agitated water, forming a loathsome circle, within which he catches an instantaneous glimpse of a white frantically struggling shape, like a big fish in a net, before the armoured jaws snap shut on their prey.

The seething commotion of the water he has never seen anything but dead calm creates a nightmare effect, crowded, horrible, chaotic, reminiscent of some ancient, over-detailed representation of the end of the world, intended to terrify and confuse the beholder. Enormous waves continue to crash on the rocks and explode in great fountains and fans of shimmering spray, while other waves race towards one another, meet and collapse in turmoil, or hurl themselves high in white water-spouts as if trying to reach the moon. Flakes of mingled blood and foam fill the air, whirling everywhere, forming a scum on the water, where the murderous long teeth, still shedding gouts of blood, flash like knives in the moonlight; which glitters too on the scales of the serpentine body, as its loops alternately sink and emerge amidst the conflicting tumult of waves.

*

The man pressed his hand to his head, which was hot and heavy. He must have dozed over his writing, for he noticed that the pages of the notebook were creased as if he'd been leaning on it heavily. After smoothing them out as well as he could, he stood up, still feeling muzzy, and went to his suitcase to get some aspirin. Since he'd never unpacked the case, its contents had got more and more jumbled and untidy each time he dived into it for something he wanted, and the aspirin bottle was not in the corner where it should have been.

Giving up the search, he poured out some water, filling the basin and plunging his whole face into it. The icy cold shock revived him slightly, but he continued to feel confused, and worried about his unaccountable drowsiness. As he always slept badly, and never by any chance in the daytime, such a deviation from his normal bodily habits seemed to indicate a profound, as yet undiscovered, disfunction.

His anxiety increased when he glanced at his watch and saw that it was already past the hour he was supposed to be at the café. There was nothing whatever to do after dark in the village, so most people went to bed early, and the proprietor had specially asked him to be on time for the evening meal so that he himself wouldn't be kept up much later than usual. Although this was the first occasion when the visitor had not been punctual, he nevertheless had a spasm of guilt.

Hastily leaving the room, he was visited by an extremely odd sensation: his overcoat felt strange to him, heavy and unfamiliar, as if he'd put on someone else's by accident – a feeling so peculiar that he again wondered uneasily if something was wrong with him. However, during the next few seconds, both the overcoat and the situation seemed to adjust themselves round him.

The ground floor of the house was divided in half by a passage, the stairs at one end, the front door at the other, and the doors of two rooms in between, one of which opened a little way, to reveal the landlady's unfriendly face, peering at him distrustfully as he passed. She didn't speak, and he was too preoccupied and in too great a hurry to do more than mutter good-evening, without pausing or really looking at her, hurrying on to the outer door and shutting it firmly behind him.

Outside, it was unexpectedly dark. The feeble street-lights, few and far between, seemed much weaker than usual, as if the electric current were giving out, their uncertain glimmer insufficient to show a new pile of stones, fallen since he last came by, into which he stumbled, almost losing his balance, and, in recovering, he happened to glance at the sky. It was heavily overcast by black storm-clouds, and instead of continuing on his way, he stood still, receiving a shock he couldn't account for from the sight of the black roof of cloud, which appeared to sag threateningly over his head like a ceiling on the point of collapsing.

But in his dream there had been brilliant moonlight. . . . He started forward as if stung as memory came flooding back, bringing a look of nausea to his face, submerging him fathoms deep in a guilty shame, blacker than the darkest night. Intense self-loathing and disgust overcame him: appalled by his own hideous conduct, he walked on blindly, seeing nothing else. The outer world was invisible to him, his inner eyes fixed inexorably on the unspeakable scenes he had just witnessed, as on some frightful atrocity film he was condemned to watch. Passing his destination without a glance, he was unaware of the proprietor's face at the window, presumably looking for him, though no attempt was made to attract his attention. No such attempt could have succeeded, in any case. He was completely absorbed in contemplating the sadism he detested so much but could never eradicate, hurrying along the dark dismal lanes as if trying to outdistance it. Yet the worst thing about it was knowing that it was inescapable . . . an infection he carried everywhere in his blood, which would last as long as his life, always liable to break out in savage demonstrations of cruelty to the girl who had such a fatal fascination for him. Never would he be able to resist the temptation of using her as a victim delivered into his hands . . . her gentle, submissive nature stimulated all that was most base in him. All the time he was being tormented by remorse and self-hatred, he still continued to suffer the other torment of those terrible last pictures ... again and again subjected to the sight of her white flesh in the moonlight, the unbearably touching fragility of her naked body....

He had no idea how long he endured this torture before gradually, by slow degrees, his surroundings began to take shape again ... but in a distorted form, as if they were visions conjured up by his disturbed mind. He didn't recognize the ruins looming round him, which appeared to be the remains of buildings larger and grander than the rest of the village, though far gone in decay, yet, in spite of their massive size, had a desolate dream-aspect and seemed to lack permanence or even precise location. A certain inevitability that was dreamlike too conducted his eyes to the terminal house of the cul-de-sac he was in, which was as lifeless and blank as its neighbours. At first he was too bemused to know what gave him the impression it might be occupied. . . . He felt strange and empty, as if he'd collapsed inwardly, as if something inside him had fallen to pieces.

With an effort he realized that a large object in front of the house was a car, and one, moreover, he had already seen ... on the carferry. At the same time he recalled the pair in whom he'd taken such an interest, but thoughts and pictures of them came back to him only evanescently, each sinking out of sight again in confusion, as the next arose from the chaos filling his head.

In the midst of these muddled recollections, it suddenly struck him that the girl living here with the car's owner was in danger and must be warned at once. He alone could do it ... nobody else knew.... He advanced towards the grim edifice with this intention, then paused, uncertain what he meant to do, taking a few steps backward until stopped by a projecting buttress, against which he leaned. A moment ago he'd distinctly seen the peasants crowded into the small smoky room, like the damned in a painting of hell. Now he couldn't remember what they were plotting ... the picture was fading already ... becoming blurred and remote ... like an illustration to an improbable story he'd almost forgotten.

All trace of it was obliterated from his memory by a pool of light as the iron-studded door opened and the man resembling a pirate emerged. The principle of distortion was still at work, making him look larger than life ... stark, savage, archetypal, a symbol of destructive force, his face carved in ferocious planes, bloodthirsty, insatiable.... When he took a gun from somebody inside the house, put it into the car and climbed into the driver's seat, the weapon seemed so much part of him that the onlooker never even wondered what he could be going to shoot in the middle of the night. Instead, he suddenly recalled the scene on the deck of the car-ferry so vividly that it seemed more actual than the present moment, with which it was inextricably confused, so that he was afraid he might be accused of prying into the other man's private affairs... spying... too interested in matters that did not in any way concern him.

To his relief, however, the driver of the Thunderbird drove off at once, not even seeing him, passing without a glance. As the car disappeared, with perfect timing, the light was extinguished; leaving him the impression that what had occurred had been a scene on the stage, though he couldn't decide whether he'd been an actor in it or a mere spectator. Now that it was over, he moved away, retracing his steps, since the road went no further. He felt more confused than ever, tired and vaguely upset, still haunted by that sense of inner collapse. His head was aching badly and seemed strangely empty – it contained no thought of his guilt, or of anything else, as he walked on without even thinking where he was going, until he suddenly found himself facing the old wall, in which there was a large breach at this point.

The sky had lightened considerably, he could see the mountains outlined against it, as well as the nearer slopes and the black masses of trees. The fiord's ghostly gleam caught his eye, and he stopped to look at it, sunk like a bowl below the level of its surroundings... a receptacle into which drained all the savage ferocity of the wild landscape.

Something evil seemed to emanate from the water, rising in steamlike mist shapes that became wraiths, meeting, separating, blending, flitting from place to place with a peculiar effect of furtive haste, accelerated by the wind, which he now noticed for the first time, swishing through a group of trees not far from him, and making a noise that reminded him of the sea, of waves breaking on some remote, lonely shore. The sound brought him a sudden new thought, and his face changed in the darkness, expressing both relief and alarm. He'd been labouring under a gross illusion in thinking about the fiord as if it were a lake. His muzziness now really perturbed him – how could he have been so muddle-headed as to forget that fiord and sea were one? His notion of a sort of sink of iniquity became ludicrous, mere melodramatic imagining, as he remembered how, every day, the water was cleared of all impurities by that great natural cleanser.... The crazy way he'd been evoking demons from the very element that was of its essence, pure and antidemonic, seemed only to be explained on the basis of some physical disability. Again he wondered whether he could be ill, although, apart from the headache, he had no symptoms, and certainly wasn't ill enough to be so mixed up. Perhaps he'd caught a chill, standing all that time in the freezing cold.... Where.? When? Why? His memory was full of great gaping holes, but his uneasiness about them was less insistent than the desire to get back to his room and lie down. Moving on again, he took the first turning that looked as if it led in the direction of his lodgings which proved to be a short cut and brought him back within five minutes.

In his dreary overcrowded room, the light was dimmer than he'd ever seen it and flickered continuously. He deliberately stood near the lamp as he took off his clothes, so tired that he let them lie where they fell among the dark, ponderous pieces of furniture, which tonight seemed to press round him inquisitively. The electricity failed finally just as he put on his pyjamas, leaving him in pitch-darkness. Reaching for the lamp, he proceeded to fumble with it, striking innumerable matches and twisting the wick up and down without producing any result. Exasperated, he seized the candle, which was also within reach; by the time he'd lighted it, the floor had turned to ice under his bare feet, and he at once climbed into bed, without waiting for the precarious flame to establish itself. But then he could find no flat surface near him where he could put the candlestick down, and as the feeble, blue-edged flicker was on the point of expiring, he let the whole thing slide out of his hand and clatter on to the floor.

Only then did it occur to him that he hadn't taken the tablets without which he was seldom able to sleep. But the effort of relighting the candle seemed beyond him, and he lay back on the pillow, meaning to rest a minute before attempting it.

The memory of his dream – if that was what it had been – had not returned to him. In the fog of his mental confusion, he was aware of it, and of its accompanying remorse, only as a faint, undefined anxiety he assigned to no special cause, which troubled him merely in a submerged and half-conscious fashion. Lying there in the dark, he soon forgot all about it, and the tablets as well, drifting over the borderline of sleep in a few moments.

All night long he continued to sleep soundly and dreamlessly, not even altering his position. It was years since he'd last enjoyed a night of such long, deep, natural, undisturbed sleep. He woke next morning feeling thoroughly rested, so much the better for it that the deficiencies of his memory sank into oblivion, completely forgotten.

10

LUZ started out of her dream with a startled cry, feeling the pirate-faced man's ungentle hands on her throat and mouth, half believing, in the confusion of waking, that he had come to kill her. She still felt confused when she understood that he wanted to keep her quiet – why should that matter in this room where no one could hear them?

'Dress quickly,' he told her. 'We're leaving at once. But not a sound – nobody must know!'

Leaving? Her wide, sleep-dazed eyes, all black pupil, gazed wonderingly at his partly seen face, above and outside the restricted radius of the lamplight, her lips soundlessly shaping 'Why?'

'It's the only chance. Every road will be jammed the moment the news spreads. . . .' Silent as a shadow, he drew back from the light and was gone.

She wasn't sure, in her bewilderment, whether she'd heard or imagined the words'. 'The ice is coming', now echoing ominously in that part of her mind where the secret dread of winter had its perpetual abode.

For a second she stood in her nightdress, still warm from sleep, watching in the great glass a pulse above her right collar-bone, which caught her eye and the light simultaneously, beating so fast that a small independent animal seemed to be struggling to burst through the almost transparent skin. The bone below it looked brittle, projecting too far; the enduring skeleton seemed to be thrusting itself prematurely through the ephemeral flesh, already dissolving in shadow and frantic beat. She was deeply disturbed by this desperate struggle going on in her own protoplasm, dissociated from consciousness; and the indescribable, undefined uneasiness if aroused continued, also below conscious level, while she put on her clothes and collected a small bag she'd been told to pack long ago with bare essentials for a sudden journey to an undisclosed destination.

The man came back for her then, not trusting her, apparently, to make no noise. His whispered 'Quiet!' startled her like a shout on the shadowy, dim-lit stairs. A shadow-figure himself, both phantasmal and threatening, he loomed over her so repressively that she forgot her questions and followed him like a sleep-walker out to the car in the freezing cold darkness.

He drove off immediately, still without speaking, skirting the sleeping village, taking a narrow road across the few fields separating the houses inside the crumbling wall from the black living wall of the forest, which seemed to press forward with ferocious vitality, as if to engulf them. Apprehensively, she watched the advancing tree-wall, a mysterious white fume smoking along its crest, like spray blowing back from the crest of a breaking wave. She'd hardly noticed the few insignificant frozen flakes drifting down as they left the house. Only now seeing, for the first time, the flickering, shimmering white thickening the air about them, she instinctively turned a dismayed face to her companion who, however, remained silent and unapproachable, merely giving her a piercing hard look out of his frigid troll's eyes, his coldly forbidding expression adding to her obscure alarm, so that she looked quickly away, not daring to ask where they were going and why.

She sat looking out at the forest, fearsomely strange with its white floor and branches furred thickly with snow, while the car filled with silence, with tension, and nameless dread. The road had deteriorated and become hard to follow. The driver seemed to have forgotten her in the effort, his set face giving the impression that he hurled the big car forward at full speed over all obstacles by a sheer effort of will. His hands on the wheel might have been gripping a cutlass – seeing them, she felt a sudden fright, a sense of alienation. She had no access to him, or to anything else in this country where everything seemed hostile, and even the forest trees conspired against her with an odd vitality, depriving her of her own.

Pallid daylight presently filtered down, the snow stopped at last. But the silence went on as if it would last for ever. The cold was all the time increasing, some freezing exudation of the black trees seeming to congeal underneath them. Nothing was to be seen but the gloomy masses of firs, the dead and the living often tangled together, often with a dead bird caught in the branches, as if deliberately. Surrounded by this vast entanglement of trees she grew more and more nervous. Trees in their millions, in battalions and armies, pressed round her on every side, their interminable ranks stretching away to infinity in all directions. Another trapped bird caught her eye, its already half-decomposed wings flapping in the wind of the car's passing, as if even so far gone in death it was struggling to get away from the murderous tree.

She shivered suddenly, the fear she'd suppressed since seeing her mirrored flesh dissolve into pulse and shadow emerging now as a conscious threat. All her hidden fears fed and magnified by this extraordinary flight, and still more extraordinary silence, she was overcome by a sudden dread of being caught by the forest like the dead bird ... of the trees weaving black branches round her in an imprisoning deadly net.

Terror forced her to look again at the man beside her, urgently and imploringly this time, twisting right round in her seat. But he ignored her and seemed totally unaware, oblivious and indifferent. His haughty features, against the white trees, looked dark and hard as if carved out of stone. His deep-set mesmeric eyes, his whole arrogant stranger's face, appeared strangely phantasmal ... the utterly alien face of a man from somewhere altogether different in time and place. All at once he looked ghostlike, inhuman, to her; entirely out of her reach. The security she had felt as his possession had become an illusion. No reassurance, no protection could be expected from him. She felt a sudden unreasoned shame at the magnitude of her mistake. How could she ever have supposed she was of any value to him?

She looked away, tears blurring the endless background of forest, already darkening towards dusk. It was as if her whole life had consisted of nothing but this eternal menacing forest, where no one else ever came, and they seemed the last two left alive on a ruined and dying planet. All day long she'd seen not a soul; so that signs of human life gave her a shock, she looked incredulously at two log huts, a gate between them blocking the road – unless it was opened they could get no further. She hardly glanced at a board with frontier regulations in three languages, her attention fixed on the gate, which was rushing towards them and had every appearance of being immovably shut. Of the sort used at level crossings, strengthened with various crossbars and reinforcements of woods, wire and metal, it was racing forward at breakneck speed, apparently invisible to the driver. She held her breath, waiting for him to put on the brake at the last moment; instead of which, without change of expression, he drove straight at it.

She ducked instinctively as the window beside her shattered, a long thin pointed sliver of glass slicing the air just over her head and embedding itself in the upholstery. There was a metallic screech, a tremendous rending, tearing and smashing; fragments of wire and wood flew about. For a timeless moment, the car swayed sickeningly on two wheels, about to turn over. She'd slipped into the corner, crushed against the door, and, clutching the edge of the seat, felt the imminent fatal crash locked in conflict with the man's will which, against all the laws of probability, eventually triumphed. By some miracle of strength or skill, or pure will-power, he brought the Thunderbird back on to its axis and drove on as if nothing had happened.

Automatically sitting up straight again, she heard, without looking round, shouts burst out behind them; a few desultory shots popped insignificantly and fell short, before the small commotion subsided and was left behind. Since the collision she'd almost ceased to think, only dimly reminded by the ice-cold wind whistling in like a continuous sequence of knives through the broken glass of a somewhat similar sound she'd once heard, or heard about, a sort of unearthly keening, made by strange forest creatures. . . . It had entangled her in a coil of dreadful events. But past and present seemed equally meaningless now, merged in one dimly receding blur. Pulling down the hood of her coat until it almost covered her face, she crouched low in her seat, while the car sped along a wider and better road.

Projecting his acute hearing beyond the sound of the engine, the man driving heard nothing. Nothing had occurred since the last shot. It was obvious they were not being followed. To be on the safe side, however, he drove on for another ten miles and as many minutes, before he pulled up, glancing at the same time at his companion. It seemed to him that she'd behaved pretty well during the recent episode, and if she'd been looking, he'd have rewarded her with a smile. As she remained huddled up as if half asleep, her face hidden by the hood, he transferred his interest to the car, which in any case was his main concern.

Snowy moorland had invaded the forest, so that the sky was again visible. Just enough light remained for him to examine the Thunderbird, remove the wire and other debris festooning it, and satisfy himself that no serious harm had been done. Pleased by the result of his inspection, he came back to his seat and informed her: 'No damage that can't be put right in half an hour.' The long preceding silence he simply ignored.

*

The girl says nothing, looking at him as if from afar. For her this is a most curious moment. She has longed for him to take some notice of her. But it's too late now, when she feels frozen, struck dumb, and he doesn't even seem human.

For a moment he keeps his eyes levelled on hers. But that compelling look of his doesn't work any more. The time seems suddenly to have gone when he could subjugate her with those eyes, trained upon her like guns, paralyzing her, stunning her into a helpless compliant doll for him to treat as he pleases. Now something comes between her and his magnetic gaze. She seems to have no feeling about him. Through the thickness of the grey coat she doesn't even feel his hand graze her shoulder when, with unheard-of concern for her comfort, he leans over to stuff his scarf in the hole in the window. To her, this unprecedented consideration seems highly unlikely, removing him even further. Their faces are close, almost touching as he leans across; she catches the cold astringent smell of his skin. Yet she still seems to see him as if from a distance, and doesn't utter a word. And he, faced with such unresponsiveness, at once turns away and drives on again, his thoughts already switched over to other things.

All she feels is a transient wonder at the sight of his cold mask profile beside her, vaguely wondering what can be going on in his head... she might as well try to guess the thoughts of a sabretoothed tiger.

Perhaps it's the after-effect of shock that's making her feel so remote and strange. In any case, whatever came between her and his eyes now divides her from everything, even herself. She doesn't seem there any longer. It's as if she has been swept up by a hurricane, carried far off towards terrifying unknown regions she can't even imagine yet. She seems to be drifting somewhere in space, a bit frightened and dizzy, but otherwise dissociated from her own being.

Then the headlights come on abruptly, calling her back, as they obliterate the last of the dying day. The car swings round a bend, passing right through a wraith of mist that happens to be in its path, dispersing the intangible stuff, which instantly constructs a different shape further off. For a second, it seems familiar to her in the artificial glare, like an incomplete, primitive sculpture she has seen somewhere before, whose fluid, changeable consistency she somehow seems to share.

11

LUKE was up so early on the first day of the voyage that patches of the deck were still wet when he began to walk round it. He was feeling unusually cheerful, as if the familiar sounds of scrubbing and hosing-down which had reached him in his cabin first thing had given the day a propitious start. He always enjoyed being at sea, and this voyage would be especially pleasant, since it was the prelude to a new life, taking him away for good from the world where he'd always felt isolated, unhappy and lost. Everything had changed now, because, for the first time, he had a definite and absorbing objective before him. Suddenly he felt a new man, confident, contented, on the verge of a worthwhile achievement at last.

He couldn't imagine why he'd taken so long to make up his mind to leave the unfriendly north and return to a certain small tropical island inhabited by an almost extinct race of large singing lemurs, known as the Indris, the study of which was to be his future life-work. This was the resolve that had made such a difference to him. As he'd always been fascinated by the Indris, it seemed inexplicable that he'd only just decided to devote himself to writing about them, instead of starting his researches long ago. However, the unaccountable delay made the prospect no less inspiring, and he strode into the cold wind feeling exhilarated, looking forward to the dedicated future which was to cancel out the lonely, dismal years he had wasted in pointless solitary travels.

He was so accustomed to being on board ship that he didn't even notice the heavy swell, his balance adjusting itself automatically as the deck tilted under his feet, without interfering with what went on in his head. His thoughts were idly dwelling on last night's embarkation scenes, when it suddenly struck him, with a considerable shock, that he remembered almost nothing of what had been happening immediately before then. At first he couldn't believe it; but it was true enough; an extreme, extraordinary vagueness affected his memory of the last few days or weeks – could it even be months? Still incredulous, he gave himself a sort of mental shake, which made no difference whatsoever . . . the fact remained that no single incident belonging to the period just over was clear or complete in his mind. He could recollect only a few scattered, inconsecutive details, and even these seemed confused and uncertain. As he considered his memory better than the average, he was quite astounded by the way recent events seemed to have been wiped out. However, this was not an appropriate moment for investigating his inexplicable amnesia, and, determined to keep his present unaccustomed sense of well-being, he deliberately started to think about other things.

Most passengers were still in their cabins this rough, blustery, cold first morning. Among the few who had emerged, he vaguely noticed a pair striding round the deck, proudly showing off their sea-legs, who now passed him again and seemed to be trying to catch his eye. Not feeling in the mood yet for becoming involved in the pseudo-friendliness of the ship's social life, he evaded them by going up to the boat-deck, which was open to the sky and completely deserted.

Some of the cheerfulness he was so resolved to hang on to seemed to have escaped already; and the remainder began to evaporate up here, where the bleak, sunless, stormy day, threatening rain, forced itself on his notice. A big sea was running. The huge, blackish corrugations of the smooth swells stretched like giant furrows to the horizon, irregularly patched with foam, under the iron lid of grey sky, beneath which separate blacker clouds were racing before the wind. Confronting the gloomy scene, he found it impossible to repress his uneasiness, or the thought of the amazing loss of memory that had caused it. A slight feeling of guilt increased his anxiety, convincing him that the forgotten period included something of special importance it was vital for him to recall. But all his efforts to remember were unsuccessful; nothing would bring it back. The gap was still just as blank when he was eventually distracted by the wind, tugging so violently at his hair and clothes that he had to retire to comparative shelter behind one of the lifeboats.

The height of this deck above the water accentuated the ship's roll. He watched the rail swing high up into the flying clouds, and then plunge down, down, down among the vast, dark, marbled, whalelike swells, which broke into a welter of foam at the touch of the hull. The hiss of the water was so loud out here in the open air that, unless he strained his ears, he couldn't hear the engines. His spirits revived as he caught the steady beat of the powerful machinery, carrying him so inevitably to the new life and work he had chosen. Nothing could stop the ship's progress, or make it turn back; nothing could prevent him from arriving at the destination he longed to reach. Slipping into fantasy, he thought how he'd get the natives to build him a hut near the forest haunts of the mysterious lemurs, where he could stay indefinitely, devoting himself to his new project without any distractions, and finding his own simple recreations when his day's work was done.

In place of the sombre seascape, his imagination provided him with a charming, childish, unrealistic scene, where branches gilded by tropical sunshine were heavy with ripe luscious fruit and brilliant with flowers. Cool jade green in the shade, sparkling diamond bright in the sun, a little stream wound through the glade, descending in a series of miniature falls to a natural swimming-pool surrounded by rocks, which the palpitating wings of enormous butterflies decorated with an exotic living mosaic. Iridescent wings shimmering round him, he dived through the rising rainbow cloud into limpid water, swimming a few strokes, floating on his back, and letting the waterfall bubble over him in a refreshing shower before he finally climbed out again. Now he stretched himself full length on the grass to dry in the sun, which was deliciously warm on his wet skin but intensified instantly to a fierce scorching blaze. In a flash, the searing heat became intolerable, so that he had to move... into the shade of an old pear tree growing beside a deserted farmhouse. At least, he seemed to be there... though he was confused by pictures of sea and jungle, which seemed to exist at the same time, giving the effect of different exposures accidentally superimposed on the same negative. Luz was lying on a sunny bank just below him, her flimsy sleeveless summer dress revealing the slight curves of her slender body. She'd clasped her hands over her eyes to shield them from the glare, so that her raised arms exposed the hollows beneath, in which minute beads of sweat showed bright on the darker surface of the shaved flesh....

The heat still seemed insufferable, even now. As he'd already removed his jacket, he could only rip open his shirt, which he did so impatiently that a button flew off as he pulled the clammy damp cotton away from his skin, to which it was adhering. Half dazed for a second, he pressed his hands over his eyes, and at the same moment heard a voice he hardly recognized as his own say with startling intensity: 'Remember that if you're ever in any trouble. . . .'

He was remotely aware of the low, urgent voice going on to finish the sentence, although it was left incomplete in his mind, as he didn't hear the last words. All his attention had suddenly been transferred to the girl, who'd twisted round to face him and was supporting her weight on her hands in a posture that would have been awkward in anyone else, but in her case merely emphasized a touching youthfulness. The simple little girl's dress she wore had a rather low neck, and, rucked up by her abrupt turn, now exposed her thighs, which, as her arms and legs were bare, produced the momentary impression that she was naked before him. . . .

Clattering crockery on the deck below indicated that bouillon was being carried round to those passengers who had ventured out. Later in the voyage, ice-cream would be substituted at mid-morning, but not until they were in much warmer waters and the ship's personnel had changed into white tropical uniforms. None of the stewards came up to the boat-deck now, doubtless assuming that people had more sense than to expose themselves to the weather there.

The squally wind had got rougher, and during the last few minutes it had started to rain. Yet for some reason Luke stood quite still until the clink of china had died away, and only then hurried under cover.

*

The day having failed to live up to its promising start, he went to his cabin early that evening. But no sooner was he lying down with a book than the idea that he'd forgotten something most important, which had been more or less submerged by what went on around him, again sprang into the forefront of his attention. Extremely perturbed now by the huge incomprehensible gap in his memory, he gave up trying to read and concentrated on attempting to recall the recent past. What on earth was the important thing he'd forgotten? Now, in addition, it seemed essential for him to remember the end of the sentence he'd spoken so urgently. But again, all his efforts were useless; he had no more success than before. No matter how hard he tried to recall them, the words and the whole complex of events remained stubbornly missing.

The book slipped off the bed, hit the floor with a thump, and immediately began to glide to and fro on the polished surface in time with the ship's rolling. Bending down, he discovered that it was just out of reach. But then he forgot it, fascinated by the motions his dressing-gown was making, swinging out from its hook with each roll, parallel to the floor, executing a staid pirouette as if in a stately ceremonial dance, before it returned to its normal place on the wall. When he detached his eyes from these moves, they went on to a window nearby. Like the old-fashioned porthole it replaced, it was fitted with an inner cover of thick, heavy glass for use in bad weather, which was now tightly screwed down. Through it he could only just discern the water outside, which looked like a continuous solid wall, except when it intermittently surged against the pane as if trying to burst its way in; while the glass calmly went on reflecting the reading-light over his bed. The dressing-gown was no longer in his field of vision, so he was astonished to see it swing out from the wall again.... Only it wasn't his dark silk dressing-gown any more, but a gigantic masculine arm, lunging threateningly out of nowhere....

Once more he watched the black, brutal, tremendous arm descend on the pitiful fragile figure, which crumpled beneath it, but not before the girlish voice had called to him piteously: 'Do you remember...?'

The words he hadn't heard properly at the time instantly restored the lost end of his own sentence, to which they related: suddenly it was obvious that Luz had tried to remind him of his promise to come and help her if she was ever in trouble....

The cabin seemed to shiver in front of him in the light of this revelation. He experienced a strange shattering shock, like an explosion, which went on reverberating in the depths of his being long after its first devastating blast. It was inconceivable that he should have forgotten... impossible to believe. Yet there was the incontrovertible fact, which could not be denied. He couldn't face the enormity of his forgetting... he refused to look into that yawning crater, deeper than comprehension... it was too fearful to contemplate. He felt a transient hopeless despair at the loss of the new purposeful individual he had so briefly been: but this was at once overwhelmed by his astounded incredulity – how could he possibly have dreamed of dedicating himself to the Indris after the promise he'd given? What devilish aberration had brought him aboard this ship, on which he'd have to stay until the next port of call?

At last he was beginning to realize something of the stupor he must have been in ever since leaving his uncomfortable, overcrowded room in the village. But his memory was still faulty, he was still partially stupefied, unable to recall the details of his departure or to grasp anything fully. All he could feel at the moment was a vast, all-embracing bewilderment and dismay, such as might be felt by a simple traveller, setting off, as he believes, on his appointed path, only to be told, days later, that it's the wrong one, and that he must go back to the starting-point and begin his journey all over again.

*

The wrong path.... He is puzzled by the complex geography of the trails between forest and fiord, until he finds that only the one by the water leads anywhere – all the others just peter out, so that, after losing himself in the trees, struggling through dead, shoulder-high weeds, clambering over boulders and down deep ravines, he always has to return finally to the same waterside track he already knows.

Tonight he seems to be out much later than usual. A full moon shines down on the savage terrain through which the path winds on and on endlessly. A recent fall of snow, sparkling with diamond prisms in the bright white light, gives the scene a wild, eerie beauty which somehow seems ominous. He tells himself he's often been here before and knows the path well, but in fact he doesn't recognize anything – certainly not this high promontory of strange upended rocks, projecting far into the fiord, and topped by a narrow platform, as if meant for high-diving.

In the fashion of dreams, without any transitional stage, he finds himself at the top of the lofty, snow-powdered rocks, and from here he can see *two* moons: one shining up from the black water to meet the white light the other pours down from the sky. The edges of the fiord are frozen. Not a ripple dims the reflected moon, and this doubled illumination shows everything as clearly as daylight, including the shivering girl, kneeling or crouching naked before him.

He stands motionless, staring down at her fixedly. The moon is so bright that he can even see the exceptionally delicate texture of her white skin. There's hardly room for them both on the platform, and she is very close to him... under his eyes... within reach of his hand.... One hand starts to move towards her, but the gesture is checked immediately. His hand hasn't really moved.

The cord loosely binding her frail wrists – which look as if they would snap at the pressure of a finger and thumb – has marked them deeply in the course of her futile attempts to escape. She has stopped struggling now. Her hands jerk occasionally like injured birds – a motion caused by the violence of the shudders convulsing her ceaselessly. Her head droops in exhaustion, she seems on the verge of collapse, her silvery hair hangs forward, concealing her face....

He presses his hand to his aching head, feeling he's going out of his mind... finding himself again in the dappled shade of the old pear tree by the empty farm, although other scenes exist too, continually changing places with one another. He still sees the girl's pathetic form in the moonlight, naked and bound at his feet; plunging down like a white shooting star to the cruel black icy water. Her fragile figure confronts him melodramatically in a stage spotlight, under the slashing blows of black shadows, twisted in agitated disarray on a grassy bank.

He can't escape her. Wherever he looks, some variation of her frail body is waiting... turning towards him a white, imploring, terrified face, framed in shining, dishevelled hair, which emphasizes her pathos and helplessness, the face of a victim of some calamity.

*

Luke passed his hand over his forehead. He was sitting up in bed in his cabin. An odd scraping noise he couldn't place, not very loud, made him look down; the book was still sliding backwards and forwards on the floor with monotonous regularity. Remembering that he couldn't reach it, he left it alone; and kept his eyes away from the window and his dressing-gown. Some compulsion seemed to prevent him from looking at anything in the outer world, drawing his attention relentlessly inwards, and focusing it on the unbelievable hiatus in his memory, forcing him to accept it as real. Once he'd done that, he had to accept the reality of everything else – of all those atrocious visions he'd just been having. It followed like a corollary that he mustn't see Luz again. The danger was too great, the evil side of his nature too strong. His sadism was the calamity to which she had fallen a victim.

While thinking this, he was all the while seeing her as he had at first, the white fire of her arresting albino's hair a flickering aureole round her head, her fragility and her almost transparent skin making a glass girl of her, a being who seemed not quite real, with the expression, both docile and apprehensive, of someone at once foredoomed and resigned, as if she accepted her fate in advance. It flashed through his mind that every girl who'd ever attracted him even slightly had had something of that same vulnerable, submissive aspect — something of the pathos of a toy, constructed only to be destroyed. But immediately afterwards he was filled with resentment and thought of nothing but protesting violently against fate. It was hideously unfair . . . he'd never wanted a victim. All he had ever hoped for was a little contact with someone to make him feel less isolated in the world. What injustice that he should have to suffer all this. How diabolical of fate to involve him with the very person who appealed so irresistibly to his sadistic impulse, which otherwise might have remained in abeyance.

His head was aching violently, as though it would burst from the conflicting pressures inside it, and without knowing he did so, he clutched it with both his hands. He felt dizzy, as though he were falling . . . a rushing noise in his ears made him think the sea must have broken through the thick glass and be pouring into the cabin . . . The ship was rolling so much he'd be thrown out of bed, to drown in the rising flood.

His mind groped for something to cling to, but he couldn't find his hands. Still clamped round his head, they remained incomprehensibly missing in this extremity . . . useless, unavailable to him.

12

THE sun is shining with a peculiar pale intensity, as if determined to condense into a brief hour or two all the light it spreads over a much longer time further south: its heatless radiance, flooding down from the cloudless, colourless sky, gives this northern city an almost chimerical aspect. The limpid brightness seems to hide more than it shows, for only a bare impression of a city emerges, its streets and big buildings suggested rather than seen. Countless polished windows reflect the sun, which flashes too on the bright metal parts of small boats and ferries, and dances and sparkles on wind-ruffled water at the end of the main street, where the harbour, shimmering like a mirage, comes right into the town.

The sun is describing so low an arc that it shines straight into people's eyes. Luz shades hers with her hand, as she hurries, half running, down the main street. But as she's facing the water, she can't help catching an occasional blinding flash from the burning snakes wriggling along the tops of the waves, which keep blazing up, bursting into sudden flames in mid-air, filling the whole atmosphere with their incessantly shattering and reviving fires.

Slightly bemused by so much dazzle and movement, she murmurs apologetically without dropping her hand, when she bumps into one of the other pedestrians she can hardly see in all the glare. Their looming shapes are mysterious, indistinct as shadows, but, contradictorily, much more solid than she, and seem to impede her, either intentionally or by accident, so that they ought really to be held responsible for the collision.

She has now almost got to her destination, a huge public building facing the sparkling water of the harbour across a wide open space. Perhaps intimidated by its sheer size, she gradually slows down as she approaches it. There's something queer about the place, which, like everything else, has the odd vagueness so much dazzle imparts; and moreover, there's something very strange about its design.

A tall windowless gable, several storeys high, towers above shallow steps rising from the street to a row of pillars; these meet at right angles a similar row of vertical uprights above an identical flight of steps, which are surmounted by another gable, looking away from the first. Each gable-wall confronts a single, separate, giant column, which stands like a punctuation mark; but fails to terminate the structure according to any accepted rule of architecture, so that the total effect is one of profound uncertainty as to where the imposing edifice begins or ends ... or how ... or even if....

The whole place seems to swell up to monstrous, impossible, dream-proportions, as she puts her foot on the bottom step ... thinking only of how to escape as quickly as possible from her conspicuous, vulnerable, exposed position on these wide steps, raised above the heads of the passers-by. At the top, she hurries through a dark entry behind the pillars, leading into an ante-room, which leads in turn into a great hall of stupendous size, dark after all the dazzle outside. She peers around nervously at the indistinct mosaics, the marble, the gold decorations she can't see properly.

Her eyes appear to get used to the dimness quite suddenly. But she sees the next moment that this isn't really what's happened, as strong light is streaming down from an unseen source, and presumably has been all along. How can she have made such an extraordinary mistake? To have imagined it was dark when it was all the time so brightly lit gives her a shock. Her grasp of reality seems to be slipping. Especially as she only now notices the grim figures in uniform standing at intervals, who all have her under observation. Her nervousness increasing, she gets the idea they are eyeing her with suspicion and wonders what she ought to do next – if only she'd found out the correct procedure beforehand....

For once she's in luck, as it happens: a stranger entering from the street shows her what to do by consulting a board on which the names of different authorities are inscribed. As soon as he moves on, she goes over to look at it, and finds she'll have to go up to the third floor. But how on earth does she get there, when there's no sign either of stairs or a lift? the watchful guards, or whatever they are, have remained still as waxworks till now: when they suddenly startle her by all pointing the same way at once in a rapid, identical, perfectly synchronized gesture. Perhaps, after all, they mean to be helpful, but somehow she doesn't think so, as she hurries in that direction – only to be confronted by a fresh problem, in the shape of a strange apparatus she has never seen in her life. With no visible means of propulsion, small boxes or cages the size of a telephone-box are rising and falling in endless sequence as if demonstrating perpetual motion. Are they meant to take people from floor to floor, and, if so, how is she to stop one? Or is she supposed to jump in while it's moving? Not seeing any directions, or any way of controlling the mechanism, she gazes at it dubiously, by no means certain that it's a lift at all.

Once again a casual arrival from outside gives her a lead, stepping into one of the boxes during the infinitesimal time it is at floor level without the least hesitation or interference with the machinery. The complete nonchalance with which he is borne aloft makes her ashamed of her uncertainty, and she takes a flying leap into the next box that arrives. After all, the thing's only a sort of escalator.... But what on earth would happen if one failed to get off and was carried right up to the very top?

Forgetting this marginal anxiety, she springs out at the third floor and opens a door opposite, leading into a great room so overcrowded that she can hardly get in. Only her exaggerated slimness enables her to slip between the people standing just inside, who, instead of pressing closer to make room for her, seem rather to be silently resisting her entry. She can't be sure of this because one of them looks at her – she doesn't catch even a glimpse of a single face; but she can't rid herself of the notion that they're all opposing her like so many inanimate objects. There really is something exceedingly odd about them: they're so silent and motionless, and so persistently keep their faces turned away from her. And how tall they are! It's as if she were closely surrounded by tall trees....

Crowds always make her nervous; she wants to rush out of the place at once. But just at this moment, the melancholy hoot of a ship in the harbour reminds her of the urgency of the business she has come to transact here, and, pulling herself together, she decides to stay. To make sure she's got everything she'll require for the coming interview, she opens her bag; but she can't move her arms in the appalling crush, and is obliged to peer down awkwardly into its dark recesses. Her money, passport, etc., all appear to be in order: and, after this investigation, there's nothing for her to do except wait, tightly jammed in the midst of the silent and faceless throng.

They hardly seem to be moving forward at all towards the presiding officials at the end of the room, whom she can't see, although she now and then hears their stern voices, which sound the reverse of encouraging; she only knows some slow progress is being made because she's not so close to the door. It suddenly strikes her that, at this rate, the place will close long before she gets anywhere near the officials, so it's futile to stay any longer. She might just as well go now and come back another day. Relieved by this thought, she looks back towards the door; but then relief changes immediately into alarm as she sees how far she is from it, and how many people intervene between it and herself. She'll never be able to push her way to the exit past all those towering, forbidding forms; which certainly won't make room for her to pass. . . .

The undefined fears, which have been at the back of her mind all the time, refuse to be suppressed for another instant. She fights against them, telling herself to keep calm – if she loses her head, she'll be done for. Why should she be frightened, anyhow? All she has to do is explain politely that she must leave the room. But somehow this seems beyond her. Acute anxiety prevents her from speaking calmly and naturally, or indeed at all. She knows that it's essential for her to say something, and yet she can't bring out a word, as if the ominous silence of the crowd has infected her.

Crushed, pressed upon from all sides, unable to move a muscle, she stares desperately at the tall shapes hemming her in. Their faces – if they have faces – remain obstinately averted, while she searches among them with feverish intensity for one single human face . . . for the face of someone who once promised to save her . . . without any such reassuring physiognomy coming to light.

Gradually panic invades her. The situation has become supernatural and horrifying – unendurable. She simply must escape somehow. Her eyes dart wildly about the huge room until they come to a window; where they remain fixed, with an expression of terror and incredulity.

Unbelievable as it seems, outside it is snowing hard. Under the black sky, a swaying, shimmering, close-woven fabric of white fills the air like a curtain shutting out everything. But that's not possible... a minute ago there was brilliant sunshine... not a cloud was in sight.... Since the weather can't possibly change so fast, she can only suppose she must have been here much longer than she thinks.

Turning her head, she looks at a big round clock on the wall beside her. Its hands are large and black, its numerals clearly marked; and yet their position means nothing to her. After staring at the clock face for nearly a whole minute, she's still none the wiser – it's precisely as though she'd never been taught how to tell the time. This discovery shocks her more than anything has so far, and completes her demoralization.

The worst thing about it is that it's all happened to her before... she knows this insane terror only too well. She has experienced already this sensation of helpless weakness, of unreality. The anguish she feels now is part of a recurring pattern, of her victim's fate, which suddenly breaks through the everyday aspect of things in a world which has never been what it seemed.... She doesn't know where she is in it any longer, or even who she's supposed to be.

These are not people crowding around her, but great, tall, threatening shapes of phantoms or trees, dark as firs in the snow, and bristling with savage hostility, terrifyingly strong. Utterly at their mercy, paralyzed, speechless, enmeshed by ghosts, she stands trapped by the white weaving snow, which has already obliterated the real world.

A new ice-age seems to be starting. Tremendous towering cliffs of solid ice, mountain-high, move down from the pole. Their terrible white glistening spearheads pierce and pulverize the highest mountains, level the Alps, engulf forests and cities, freeze oceans with all their fish and whales, crush out the life of the planet.

Smooth, shining, unearthly, without a break, the white walls loom all round her, a vast, glacial, nightmare encirclement, implacably closing in.

The light of day fades in its eerie dazzle. All is distorted, phantasmal. In the dead silence, the weird, iceberg-glittering mirage-light of this colossal circuit no trace of reality can penetrate.

Imprisoned within the impassable walls of the locked, lifeless polar world, all that is left for her is a deathly cold isolation, numbing her senses and freezing her brain. The world lost, the light lost, the mind lost, the coldly gleaming, relentlessly moving ice has become her sole and final reality.

13

THE ship wasn't moving in any direction, merely wallowing in heavy swell. It was early morning and exceedingly cold; unnaturally cold for the latitude and the season, according to which it should have been daylight, even at this hour. Yet all was black as midwinter outside the portholes of the captain's cabin; the dim light mainly illuminated the owner's bald head and the papers outspread before him, over which he stooped with both hands flat on his desk, simultaneously conversing inaudibly with a colleague.

There was an abbreviated knock and the passenger entered, without waiting to be called in. The other two looked up sharply, their hostile disapproval felt rather than seen, since their faces were almost hidden, so heavily were they muffled against the cold. Their sole response to the newcomer's greeting was a couple of grunts; after which they resumed their muttered confabulation as if still alone.

Checked in his intended leave-taking, the passenger stopped in front of them, the centre of a circle of isolation. He was aware of their antagonism but too remotely to be affected by it. His mental state just then was slightly abnormal, the sleeping-tablets he'd taken too recently for their effect to have quite worn off were confusing his thoughts, and he still felt muzzy from last night's farewell drinking.

Remembering how late he'd gone to bed after the party, he experienced one of his not infrequent spasms of self-dislike and contempt. Why couldn't he resign himself to his isolation, instead of making these futile, undignified, periodic attempts to pretend it didn't exist? How ridiculous, how despicable he must have appeared to the other people last night . . . how they must have laughed at his asinine efforts to seem one of them.

The disgust he felt for himself didn't last this time, but dissolved next moment in his general vagueness, leaving him without a single definite thought in his head. He was still standing in the same place, bemused, when the captain abruptly looked up to ask whether he'd changed his mind about going ashore – a question too superfluous, in his opinion, to need an answer; though the harsh voice paused as if one was expected before adding, in a tone the reverse of friendly, 'All I can do then is wish you luck.'

It sounded more as if he wished him in hell, but they both automatically started the gesture of shaking hands, abandoning it at once as if by mutual consent, the captain resuming his previous mutterings.

There was no further reason for the passenger to remain; by rights he should have now left the cabin. For some reason, however, it didn't occur to him to move, and he stayed where he was, suspended, staring at nothing in particular, as if half asleep. When a slight movement behind the two mumbling forms drew his eyes to a third man in uniform he couldn't identify in the deep shadow, his vague ruminations began to revolve around the question of whether this person could have come in without his noticing, or had been there all along. Nobody spoke to him. But the increasingly tense atmosphere, and the sombre looks surreptitiously aimed at him, indicated that he was the object of a unanimous enmity, the cause of which was not clear. The captain, apparently, could hardly wait for him to go. Growing more impatient each second, often interrupting what he was saying to stare insistently at him, he finally burst out uncontrollably: 'How much longer are you going to hold us all up?'

Since there couldn't have been any delay so far, his exasperation seemed excessive, inexplicable, to the passenger who, at the same time, suddenly grew aware of his own muddle-headedness and aimless loitering and hurriedly left the cabin with a muttered apology, followed by the man from the background, whom he now recognized as the chief officer.

The cold became more intense as they reached the deck, on which snow was steadily falling. Letting the other pass, the traveller paused in bewilderment, wondering what could have happened to the climate. A dim suspicion that he'd been brought to the wrong place seemed so fantastic that he at once lost sight of it in the snow's complex fluctuations.

The countless snowflakes, eddying in the wind, created a curious foglike gloom in the upper air, excluding daylight almost completely, swarming round the few lights and reducing them to the feeblest glimmer. The small flakes came crowding down persistently, inexhaustibly, as if they would go on without ever ceasing, falling for weeks... months... years.... This was just how they'd been falling last night, and they certainly hadn't stopped since for a single second.

Noticing that the officer was already almost hidden from sight, he shook himself into motion, groping after him, forced to go carefully to avoid colliding with various parts of the ship's superstructure, which became visible only when they loomed up, glistening with ice, just in front of him. Looking about with vague expectancy, he caught the tail end of the thought that some of last night's drinking companions might be coming to see him off; and, disgusted all over again by the absurd self-delusion, he made a resolute effort to clear his head. But the numbing cold wasn't conducive to mental activity: the wind driving the snow against him seemed to blow straight off the polar ice.

Bearlike in many wrappings, a seaman lumbered past with his suitcases in mysterious silence – all footsteps were soundless on the snowy deck. The silence, now that he'd noticed it, seemed uncanny, uncannily emphasized by the continuous low throbbing under his feet. The faint sound initiated a new train of thought, and sent him hurrying after his escort, whom he addressed for the first time in a voice that sounded surprised: 'The engines – they haven't stopped...'

'You bet they haven't! The skipper can't wait to turn about. He's been cursing you for days for making us put in here.' The words were maliciously spoken, with the same unexplained animosity that had been so noticeable in the captain's case, though this man couldn't control his curiosity, asking: 'Why *have* you come, for God's sake?'

'I have to find someone.'

The frigid, curt voice prohibited further questions or comments, and, without exchanging another word, they arrived at the rail, which was thickly encased in ice, and had a rope-ladder dangling down from it towards the invisible water. Hearing the sound of a motor down there, the mystified passenger leaned over the side, but saw only the involved, ever-changing patterns of the snow.

'Harbour's frozen over. They can only keep open a narrow channel, so we've got to put you ashore by launch.' Having supplied this information, the officer swung one leg over the rail and descended the ladder with practised ease, not offering any assistance.

Luke followed him awkwardly. He needed both hands to cling to the rope, so that the snow blinded him and he didn't see who pulled him into a rocking boat; where he immediately became a target for hostile stares, as if all those manning it had a personal grudge against him, though he didn't notice this either. Nor did he see a hand reach out to push him towards a seat, into which he went sprawling, as the launch instantly shot forward at full speed.

He had difficulty in keeping his balance even while he was sitting down, for the small boat plunged and reared like a bucking horse and bounced wildly from swell to swell, sheets of spray flying over the tiny cabin. And, in the midst of all this violent chaotic motion, he remained unaware of the grim, obdurate faces around him.

The ship they'd just left had already vanished into the blizzard. It had been cold *there*, but it was a thousand times colder down here on the water. The cold was brutal, paralyzing: he'd never felt anything like it.

The sky was invisible, still blurred and darkened by the queer snow-fog, against which the white falling flakes wove their continually changing designs like an intricate, fluid lace. He stared at these complexities so long that they began to assume peculiar shapes – distorted forms of mermaids and men, pallid masks of the drowning or drowned. To exclude them, he covered his face with his hand, sinking into a kind of daze of cold and discomfort.

He was roused suddenly by an extraordinary long-drawn-out yell, which was really more of a howl and sounded alarmingly close, although nothing could be seen through the welter of snow and spray. Jumping up, the officer shouted back unintelligibly through a megaphone, and after several exchanges resumed his seat with the laconic remark: 'One-way traffic.'

Luke looked at him blankly, not understanding, then followed his gesture towards a distant indistinct commotion, which gradually defined itself as a spectral ship, motionless as a rock by contrast with the frantic activity of the crowd of small boats seething round it, all struggling desperately to get near enough for their occupants to climb aboard, each for himself at the expense of the rest, all the time jostling, ramming and even capsizing each other in their mad, panic-stricken, relentless competition, at which the passenger gazed in horror.

Although the launch steered clear of the frenzied mêlée, he couldn't help hearing the confused hubbub of shouts, screams, thuds and splashes pursuing them long after the scene itself had been left behind, finally turning to his escort with an unspoken query – what could be happening here?

He was told: 'You know as much as I do – you heard the news. How people are fighting to get away, crazy to get on to any ship that'll take them. We've got room for a few ourselves. But the old man won't wait long enough to pick them up.'

Abruptly the violent movement stopped, speed dropped to dead slow, and the speaker, interrupting himself, hurried outside and remained there, calling down incomprehensible steering directions at intervals.

Left alone with his remembered disturbing vision of battling small craft, Luke was distracted from it only when an oscillating gust caught the opaque fabric of snow, lifting it to give him an astonishing glimpse of his surroundings. They were in a channel between ice-fringed walls, beyond which extended a waste of white hillocks and hummocks that was the frozen harbour. The monotony of so much white had a baffling effect on his eyes; he couldn't judge the size of the abandoned hulks, dotted about like houses, immovably embedded in the thick ice, and almost believed he'd imagined them, when the white curtain came down again, blotting everything out, even the icy walls that were nearly close enough for him to touch with his hand.

It was as though he had dreamed that arctic scene. And he assumed the weak, flickering lights that next appeared in the distance were some sort of optical illusion, coming and going continuously, like will-o'-the-wisps, in the vicinity of the unseen horizon. They couldn't possibly be real. Real lights would have got bigger and brighter as they approached; whereas these were just as dim and evanescent when presently the launch stopped moving, and the officer put his head into the cabin to announce their arrival.

*

The traveller at once gets up and goes out: but then stops and stands motionless, clutching the roof of the cabin and staring ahead. The lights are invisible at the moment. He sees only the eternal snow, now falling even more heavily and in larger flakes, which settle on his shoulders like weightless birds.

The suspicion of having been brought to the wrong place again crosses his mind. He can't believe this is his destination. Not a building is to be seen, there's absolutely no sign of a town. All he can make out is the immediate foreground, with a flight of steps coming down to the water from the sea-wall, which has an iron ring cemented into it. One of the crew inserts a boat-hook into this ring, pulling the launch alongside, while another jumps out with his suitcases, deposits them at the top of the steps, and returns at the double.

By the time the seaman resumes his place, the passenger has ceased to see anything whatsoever, overtaken by absence and vagueness, as he was in the captain's cabin, unaware that everybody on board is staring at him fixedly, waiting for him to move. As they lean forward in tense watchful poses, their faces express the utmost hostility and infuriated impatience, in striking contrast with his own blind, blank look. Tension mounts in a rapid crescendo in the glacial hush, which the indifferent pulse of the motor hardly disturbs. The dreamer remains oblivious of the faces round him . . . if he suddenly saw their murderous expressions he'd surely think they were part of the nightmare by which he's immobilized.

As the seconds pass and he still stands there, the sailors grow more and more enraged, starting to mutter among themselves, truculently, vituperatively . . . the officer decides it's high time he took charge of the situation, and he does so by seizing the other man's arm, meaning to drag him ashore by force.

His threatening grip instantly recalls Luke to himself. Shaking it off, he says, as if to explain, or even to make a joke of his hesitation: 'It was so damned cold sitting still in the boat. I was frozen stiff . . . couldn't move for a second.' He actually contrives a wry smile, then, without further delay, jumps on to the steps, feeling at the last moment his familiar desire for acceptance, approval. He wants to make a normal impression, to speak and act as he believes other people would in his predicament. But the attempt is a failure; his behaviour seems false and serves only to remind him of his real isolation.

The launch has already shot off, and disappears now in churning white whirlpools where snow meets spray. The waves of the wake chase each other along the channel, swelling over the lower steps, subsiding quickly to mere surface undulations, which soon cease altogether; while he stares down in amazement at a strange silky film forming on the blackish water, which is freezing visibly.

The motor of the receding boat is no longer audible. Suddenly he grows aware of vast silence and loneliness all about him. When he turns away from the water, he seems to be facing a wide open space, uniformly flat, white and empty, the boundaries of which are lost in the falling snow. Deep snow already covers the ground, on which millions more flakes hurriedly settle each second. Nothing suggests the proximity of a town . . . or of anything else. . . . He is reluctant to advance into that forbidding cold vacancy. The silence, the emptiness, the total absence of any sign of life, seem alien and unnerving.

Now, however, the elusive lights reappear, and instinctively he starts towards them, since they are the only indication that human beings exist anywhere near him, quite forgetting his luggage, which has already become indistinguishable from the white background. Walking proves unexpectedly difficult, his progress is very slow. The blizzard slams the frozen snow into his face as he battles against it. The countless white dots, ceaselessly surging out of the dark hole where the sky ought to be, seem to increase the slight mental confusion that has never left him. Veering all round the compass, the wind whirls them at him, first from one side, then from the other, or sends them showering down in utter chaos from all sides at once, until his head starts to spin round with them. The distant lights seem as remote as ever, coming and going bewilderingly, reminding him of old tales of travellers lured to destruction in bogs and quicksands. The marsh lights in those old ghost stories always stayed far away . . . and, like them, the glimmers ahead of him keep vanishing too, always reappearing in a different spot, as if deliberately trying to mislead him. . . .

His footsteps become slower and more laboured . . . he's gradually being worn out by the cold and the effort of struggling on. It seems a long time since he started walking. . . . But there's still nobody . . . nothing . . . only the everlasting snow, inexhaustibly falling, encircling him like a round white curtain that keeps pace with him as he moves, but doesn't prevent him from knowing he is the centre of a huge unseen emptiness, reaching to infinity on all sides.

With no obstacle to break its force, the wind is charging fiercely across the plain, driving the snowflakes straight at him, parallel with the ground. Suddenly it starts whirling them round him in crazy spirals so violent that he has to stand still, his head down. At once he feels frightened and dizzy, lost in this dreadful inhuman whiteness where nothing is to be recognized. In his confusion, he actually wishes he'd never left the steps, which were at least identifiable ... the one place that had some definition ... where human beings had been....

When the wind abates slightly, it's all he can do to move forward again. It's a terrible aching effort to keep on walking. Snowflakes seem to be whirling round in his head. The snow has become an illness, his own and the world's, the sick sky endlessly vomiting its white flux. A knot of pain forms in his head, with which the snow intermingles – suddenly his pain and the snow are one, locked together like lovers, heaving and swaying ... rocking and rolling deliriously....

A nameless disorder has invaded the world. Gangrenous, distended with frozen wind, puffed by white swellings, the sick ground seems to wince and shudder and undulate strangely. On the periphery of his vision, the snow starts to coagulate. Shapeless, churning white revolves on itself to create a miracle of erectness ... the incredible upright shape of a human form. A kind of bright shiver goes through him, as, out of the vortex, comes a figure he knows....

At once the snowflakes grow bigger, more elongated, and fall more thickly, clotting into an opaque screen through which he can hardly see the frail ghost-girl approaching him. Snow wraps her round like a garment, less bright than her hair. The apparition makes him forget his tiredness. Longing to see her more clearly, he repeatedly parts the falling snow in a swimmer's gesture, not noticing when his hands lose all sensation. Blinking away the heavy flakes that catch in his lashes, he frowns, his intent, screwed-up eyes strain in the effort to penetrate all the white dots swarming madly between them. Even now she's quite close, he can't see her at all distinctly. Their two figures remain separate, disconnected. No contact is possible while the snow shimmers down between them like spray and relentlessly keeps them apart.

Suddenly the wind shifts, blowing it out in great fans, beyond which the girl grows fainter still, more wraithlike, less substantial, until she's no more than a phantom, an unclear vision conjured out of the storm ... the snow's brightness, refracted through her, gives her a spectral transparency. He tries to call, 'Stay with me! Please don't leave me!' But before his frozen lips shape the words, a furious arctic blast falls upon him, filling his eyes with water, so that her half-seen face splinters in brittle fragments.

Her spun-glass hair ripples fanwise, grows longer and whiter still, becoming indistinguishable from the snow. White flakes flicker among the shreds of her disrupted image, which is finally swept away by the wind.

Icy needles of pain transfix him, piercing his eyes... their empty and bleeding sockets glare vacantly at the dark, where there's nothing left... no town, no lights... no ghost of love.... He is alone with his isolation, with the everlasting snow and the bludgeoning wind, which attacks him suddenly with a shriek... with a strident, unearthly howl....

Blast after murderous polar blast sends him reeling, agonizingly lashing his face. Blind, dazed, bent double, he staggers and falls into a darker and deeper night... a bottomless crevasse of blank emptiness.

14

FEW visitors ever found their way to this obscure tropical island resort, but, for the benefit of those who did, a small hotel had been built on the beach, surrounded by several cabins that were used as sleeping-quarters. Made of bamboo and a tough substance woven from palm leaves, all these huts were alike, consisting of a bedroom with bathroom behind, and a wide veranda which served as an outdoor sitting-room, overlooking the so-called garden, where a few flowering plants straggled between the palms. Then came a long row of sand-dunes, stretching both ways as far as the eye could reach, hiding the ocean and muffling the noise of the surf. Because of their height, which exceeded that of the cabins, the sandhills were generally thought to detract from the amenities of the place; but they compensated for restricting the view by acting as a protective barrier against the high tides and storms that would otherwise have threatened it at certain seasons.

At the back, the palms grew much closer together, intermingling with dense bushes and tall forest trees in an impenetrable equatorial tangle. Yet impenetrable was not the right word, for a road had been hacked through the solid, indestructible-looking vegetation, and was the only approach to the hotel, widening in front of it to form a parking place, and give cars room to turn. A year or so previously this dirt road had been improved by the addition of two narrow, tarred, parallel strips, the same distance apart as the wheels of a car; which now needed repairs in so many places that they constituted more of a hazard to motorists than a convenience.

However, the native driver employed by the proprietor was perfectly familiar with the idiosyncrasies of the route he travelled several times weekly in the course of his duties. Always a bit of a dandy, today he was looking especially elegant and debonair in green and gold silk; completing the ensemble by picking a scarlet hibiscus as he strolled to the car, twisting it into his hair, and then flinging a light European jacket over his brown shoulders in a careless gesture.

Lunch was over, and most of the staff had collected to watch him go, envying his control of the powerful American car, and his freedom to show off when he got to the town – the last based on a misconception, for he'd been ordered to come straight back immediately with the visitor who was expected to arrive by steamer. His only chance of showing off, therefore, was here and now, in front of his present audience. And he took full advantage of it, driving away at high speed, demonstrating his skilful steering by effortlessly keeping the wheels on the tarred strips with one hand, while he waved a casual goodbye with the other.

The Cadillac disappeared in the dusty haze at the bend of the road, terminating the small stir its departure had created; and, yawning, in ones and twos, the servants drifted towards their quarters for the afternoon siesta.

Now the hot, heavy, seemingly lifeless hush peculiar to this time of day envelops the hotel and its dependencies, broken only by the intermittent clash of palm leaves in the wandering wind, and the softer, more regular cough of the waves breaking beyond the dunes. Nothing moves. No living creature is visible anywhere – no dog or lizard; no bird, either of sea or land. Even the many insects are stilled by the soporific heat, which seems to subdue the very colours of flowers and sky.

The driver would have been flattered to know that someone besides his compatriots was interested in his journey. As usual, most of the cabins were empty. But one was occupied by a young woman who'd just retired there, and, instead of lying down, she went straight into the shuttered bathroom and opened the door used by the servants – not so wide as to catch the attention of anybody outside, but enough to give free access to every sound. Thus she was able to note the exact moment when the car set off on its long drive, and listen to its gradually dwindling hum, until this finally was extinguished.

Even then she didn't move or shut the door, which was so heavily overshadowed by the black living wall just outside that scarcely any light entered. In the dimness, her whitish hair had a ghostly gleam, as she continued to stand in a listening posture, although the only sound was the intermittent rattle of palm leaves, even the sea's heavy breathing being inaudible on this side.

Several tedious moments dragged past before her straining ears at last caught the expected sound (which only someone listening intently for it would have noticed): the very faint buzz of a rapidly receding car, already far inland. From her own observation, she knew how the narrow road ran for a considerable distance across flat, fertile fields, before beginning to climb the sharp-pointed foothills, whose steep slopes were now throwing back and magnifying sufficiently for her to hear the engine noise which had previously been lost among the low-lying rice fields. It soon died away. But she waited until she was perfectly sure it was not going to be heard again before quietly closing the door and going to lie down, first removing her three flimsy garments.

Stretched out flat on the bed's palm-leaf webbing, her pale, thin, somewhat underdeveloped body kept so still that it might have been laid out there, lifeless. But presently she moved to look at the time, trying to estimate in her mind how far the car would have got by now; a movement and exercise she repeated at intervals, in the obsessional manner characteristic of anxiety states, all the while half aware of the dull, ominous pounding of the surf on the beach in the background.

*

Here, practically on the line of the equator, the sea was smooth, dazzling, pellucid, pearly; colourless but for mysterious aquamarine shadings that came and went like footprints left by invisible beings strolling about on the water. No division being apparent between sky and sea, the antiquated steamer, zigzagging from one island to the next, seemed to float in mid-air, looking incredible, ponderous yet unreal, and totally inappropriate to the boundless, burning translucence in which it moved. These pure, serene, elemental transparencies seemed profaned by the noise and smoke of the engine, and by the chattering passengers crowding the deck with their friends, families and paraphernalia, among a sprinkling of motionless, stern, aloof or indifferent priests.

The solitary European on board looked as detached as the holy men squatting near him. Apparently oblivious of his surroundings, he paid no more attention to the scavenging seabirds diving and skirmishing round him than to the rowdy Coca-Cola drinkers, whose empty bottles periodically sailed past his head on their way into the sea.

His destination appeared, mirage-like, on the horizon, its central mountains wreathed in perpetual cloud – secret, still almost unexplored mountains, covered in dense jungle, they were the home of countless legends of ghosts and demons besides that of the weird singing creatures, whose abode they were said to be. Skirts swished, sandals clicked, bare feet thudded across the deck, as a general move was made to his side to see the distant island. Ignoring the crowd, he never budged from the post at the rail he had taken up hours ago in a patch of shade from the bridge. From time to time the shade moved an inch or so with the ship's slightly changing course; and whenever this happened he too made a fractional movement to avoid being exposed to the blistering sun straight over his head – otherwise he remained motionless.

His thoughts never left the pale fragile girl he was going to meet, who had occupied them ever since he woke before dawn, though not in any fresh or constructive way. Indeed, the only difference between his present inconclusive thoughts, which engendered nothing but more uncertainty, and all the preceding ones, was that he'd now equated his negative attitude towards her with his general failure as a human being. Without knowing how he'd reached this conclusion, he was convinced that only by a full and open acceptance of their relationship could he establish his identity as a real person. Yet, in spite of this conviction, in spite of having followed her all this way, he still wasn't sure what he wanted to do about her, and felt more alarmed than anything by the prospect of their meeting. It seemed so long since he last saw her that he couldn't suppress the furtive idea that everything ought to be over between them. Once upon a time he had envisaged for himself a supremely satisfactory dedicated existence.... But how unfair to blame her for turning it into a glimpse of unattainable paradise.... Ashamed, he tried to concentrate on the attraction she had always had for him; but his memory picture proved so elusive that he couldn't even see her face distinctly in his mind. Suddenly, then, it struck him that he never *had* seen her as she really was, but only in the role he had imposed upon her ... as a sort of unreal blessed innocent ... a lamb led to the slaughter ... viewing her always from the privileged position of her executioner....

For an instant her victim's image branded its burning excitement upon his nerves. Next moment he felt lacerated, he could have thrown himself overboard, genuinely shocked and appalled because he'd used their relationship as a kind of psychological masquerade for the indulgence of his own sadism. Yet, only a second later, he seemed exonerated by the thought that it was she who had loosed the sadistic demon in him . . . a cloud of pretence and confusion obscured his brain, concealing his past acts and motives. By thinking of her as if *she* was a demon in the process of destroying *him*, he gave his attitude the definition it had hitherto lacked – of course he didn't want to see her, and began to consider how best to avoid the meeting. It should be easy: he had only to stay where he was and let the ship take him on to another island. But suppose she came to the port to meet him? Supposing she actually came aboard? And now, with hideous clarity, he saw himself hiding below, sweating with apprehension in the stifling heat of his airless cabin . . where he wouldn't be safe for two seconds . . . some officious fool was bound to bring her straight to him there. . . .

The picture was insufferable. Too undignified. Too unedifying. He dismissed it from his mind. But it was beyond his power to imagine the alternative, which therefore seemed all the more unnerving, and equally unendurable. Yet one or the other he must face; there was no escape.

Outwardly as calm and aloof as ever, he began to feel almost frantic with indecision as he watched the island grow larger, close enough now for the figures on the waterfront to be seen distinctly. Below the clouds, he could even make out individual trees in the dense jungle which covered the mountain slopes in a minute, burnished, emerald patterning, like shagreen. Among the gaily dressed group assembled to welcome the arriving passengers, people were already waving in frenzied excitement. The ship's siren gave a piercing shriek, and every dog on the island started barking hysterically. At the same moment, a single puff of smoke soared high into the sky, trailing its transparent shadow across the deck. The engines stopped, the boat stopped moving, and without the faint breeze stirred up by its motion, the afternoon heat fell upon him like an oppressive weight.

Zero hour had arrived, and he still didn't know what to do. His heart had started to beat uncomfortably fast. He pressed his hand to his forehead and brought it away wet – more on account of his uncertainty, he felt, than the heat. The gangway crashed down, and immediately the chaos on deck became indescribable. Everyone was shoving and shouting at once, the whole disorderly crowd seething around him, so that he'd have been swept away from the rail by the solid mass of struggling humanity if he hadn't clung to it so tightly that his knuckles stood out like bleached bones under the taut skin. Apart from this effort, he still contrived to dissociate himself from what was happening, and didn't move, looking away from the surging mob to the tropical sunshine, which blazed down dazzlingly on the water, casting dense black shadows on land.

A few rowing-boats had already appeared round the ship and were rocking gently on the brilliant water, which was tinged yellow by the sandy floor of the harbour, and wore, like medals on its full, burningly bright breast, weird wreaths and circular clusters of pallid seaweed. Further out, the open sea rippled a darker, purpler blue, meeting the yellowish harbour water in a line so straight that it might have been ruled, while the mirror-haze just beyond was alive with flotillas of flimsy sailing-boats skimming along like white butterflies, in a breeze conspicuously absent from the shore.

Having observed all this without really seeing anything of it, he looked more attentively at the water's edge, where he was thankful to see no one he recognized, and nothing of interest. He was beginning to experience an incipient relief when, with startling suddenness, a big American car swept round the end of a row of warehouses, sounding its horn continuously, scattering people to right and left, and pulled up with a flourish right opposite him. Its only occupant was the native driver, who emerged in a leisurely fashion, strolling across to the end of the gangway, where he stood in a somewhat consciously nonchalant pose, a scarlet hibiscus flower tucked jauntily behind one ear, watching the passengers disembark.

The man on the boat groaned aloud – a small despairing sound lost immediately in the general din – and, in a last desperate attempt to decide what to do, raised his eyes, as if unhopefully imploring heaven to send him a message. But nothing unusual was visible overhead. He saw only a pair of frigate-birds sailing past, opening and shutting their tails like scissors; banking steeply against the molten sky, they swept back again in a wide curve, one of them circling round slowly, hardly moving its long wings, while the other settled on top of the mast, where it remained quite motionless, as if it had been stuffed and put there as a decoration. The big, black, fierce-looking birds of prey were common in this part of the world, and no pronouncement of any sort could be read into their appearance; so, unable to go on staring into the blinding glare, he lowered his eyes to the car which had just driven up. Undoubtedly it was the hotel car, and had been sent to meet him.

Message or not, he now discovered with faint surprise that a change had taken place in his outlook during the last few moments. The pandemonium on board was subsiding, only a few passengers were still pressing towards the gangway, and he at last moved to join them without either reluctance or apprehension, no longer thinking *she* would be at the hotel and that he'd soon have to face her – indeed, this had ceased to seem true. He might really have been the recipient of a wordless message to the effect that his meeting with Luz would not take place, and that she'd have left the hotel by the time he got there.

*

Dressed again after her siesta and holding a comb in her hand, the young woman who occupies one of the hotel's beach huts stands in front of a mirror hung on the wall. Her lustrous pale hair, slightly disordered after its contact with the pillow, looks too heavy for her extremely slight, almost childish form, which it seems to weigh down, pouring over her shoulders in a silvery flood. It appears particularly abundant because she has washed it today; besides, it's really much longer and thicker than usual, as there's no one on this remote tropical island to cut it for her. The islanders wouldn't do so even if they could. Though of course she doesn't know how her albino hair fills them with terror, white being for them a demonic colour, so that nothing would induce them to touch it, and they think she's a witch – hence the horrified glance she received from the houseboy she asked to help her rinse it.

She vaguely wonders why he turned and fled, as she now plunges the comb into the silver mass, through which she has to tug it at first, encountering less resistance each time she repeats the action, until the lustrous strands end by falling obediently in their customary sleek curves. But even now the hair, especially soft and light after its recent washing, still stirs at the slightest movement, the surface hairs continually quivering with tiny motions imperceptible in themselves, which produce the effect of surrounding her head with a tremulous silvery cloud.

She goes out on to the veranda in front of the cabin and sits down there with a book. At her feet, a few steps lead down to the garden, where a prostrate plant spreads a thick mat brilliant with orange trumpets she doesn't see, since, from the higher level, her eyes automatically cross the sunk garden to the sandhills beyond, where there's nothing to hold her attention. She isn't concentrating on the book either. Motionless and unoccupied, she gazes straight before her, except when from time to time she lowers her eyes to her watch. Apart from this minimal move, she is utterly still, with a stillness the reverse of relaxed, which suggests an acute suspense.

Still there is no life, no movement, about the hotel. The waves keep up their continuous muttering, but the palm leaves rattle at longer and longer intervals, as the wind gradually sinks with the setting sun. In the shade of the dense trees behind the main building, large drum-shaped containers have been put out to await removal by a truck which will collect them during the hours of darkness; and these tightly sealed cylinders containing the day's garbage presently attract an emaciated stray dog, which persistently sniffs and limps round them on three legs, until finally it slinks away, defeated. But this solitary manifestation of life is outside the girl's field of vision.

The air grows steadily heavier, hotter and more oppressive. With a characteristic gesture, she gathers her hair in one hand and lifts it for a second to cool her neck; and, as she lets the soft shimmering mass fall back, the sun dips behind the dunes, and the intervening hollow at once fills with shadow.

Dusk doesn't exist in this part of the world, the light starts to fade immediately. Her hair glints like water, swirling on her shoulders, as she suddenly swings round to face inland, having just caught the first faint fugitive mechanical sound of the returning car, still a long way off. Travelling downhill on the return trip, it is soon crossing the flat land, coming rapidly nearer, the volume of noise increasing each second. Still she remains, as if petrified, in that uncomfortable, twisted pose, listening to the hum of the engine, until its rising pitch fills her ears and the whole world. In a moment now, the car will reach the hotel – she knows this, not only by the sound, but from the increasing sense of urgency and approaching climax pervading everything around her.

Suddenly jumping up, she hurries down the steps and across the garden, passing between the dunes to emerge on the beach beyond, which is still in sunshine. The long curve of white sand is completely deserted, as it always is unless visitors from the hotel have come down for a swim, as the islanders consider the beach unholy and never go near it, believing that demons live in the sea. The girl is now out of sight of the hotel. Iridescent spume floats in the air like a ghostly rainbow, drifting in from the breakers, whose muted crash on a far-out reef drowns the noise of the car. A slight, solitary figure on that long empty beach, she walks at the edge of the demon-infested sea, dangling her sandals from one hand, on the wet sand which doesn't retain her footprints for half a second. Pink where it reflects the sunset, the dry, untrodden sand stretches ahead for miles, white as snow. The last slanting rays of the setting sun outline her head with brilliance, caught in the shining mass of her hair that shifts in silver eddies with every step.

The sun is so low now that it seems to rest on the rim of the sea which, in an instantaneous snap human eyes are too slow to follow, grabs the fiery ball in its jaws, swallowing it down into the maw of darkness. At once the shallows turn milky and opalescent, while further out deep water darkens to indigo in preparation for the approaching night.

*

The lonely stroller has reached a hollow, which may be the bed of a roaring torrent when rains flood down from the mountains. She looks up and is suddenly frightened, seeing the waves above her. Sudden terror invades her, the horror of icy walls implacably rising.... The fearful shape of her impending fate, closing in, hangs over her like an imminent murder... and she is trapped by it. The glassy incoming wave meets the pale piled-up sand to form a complete circle, within which she is imprisoned. The sea noise suddenly grows louder... an ominous loud booming....

As if obeying an order, she fixes her eyes on the point where the water's transparent wall joints the segment of sand... where a man's familiar face now appears... now his whole body... entering the double prison which confines her... to be irrevocably shut in with her.

He stops. Time stops with him. The poised, motionless silhouette terrifies her afresh by its immediacy, so close to her, unmistakable, even though indistinct in the failing light.

She is speechless, immobilized by the unaccountable guilt she always feels in the presence of this man. In some mysterious, almost magical fashion, she seems to have been involved with him ever since time began... and yet he's a stranger of whom she knows only that he is a danger to her and a constant threat. From what dark place of chaos, with what evil intention, is he approaching now?

A sudden uncanny light touches the stern mask face with uncanny whiteness, turning it into a statue's. It doesn't look like a man's face any longer but like an effigy in white stone. The waves break behind her with the sound of a succession of warning cries. She has the momentary illusion of watching a sculptured Mercury poised above her, bringing his message of doom. That pallid menacing shape belongs to a different category of beings... another world altogether. No contact between them is possible... they should never have met... could never meet... and yet they have met – that's what's so appalling. She has done nothing... and yet she has committed a crime, just by being with him. Simply for them to be together constitutes an offence in itself.

Horrific mysteries loom around her like the walls of a labyrinth, in which the two of them are trapped without hope of escape... both wandering, lost, there, and bound eventually to stand face to face. Something irremediable will then happen... something unbearable... something she must avoid at all costs....

In a sudden new spasm of terror, she turns and starts running in the only direction she *can* run away from him – towards the monstrous encircling wave, towering sky-high, its crest already beginning to bend and break... its whole concave glistening bulk about to crash down upon her.

15

LUKE absently passes his hand over his head, vaguely aware that it has started aching. He feels slightly bewildered, as if waking suddenly in an unfamiliar place, and looks up, half expecting to see a big bird, a stuffed one possibly, somewhere over his head. Instead, he finds himself surveying a slatted ceiling in need of repair, where lizards of assorted sizes are frisking about, whisking their flexible tails. The big, bare, shabby room is full of the noise of surf, so that huge breakers seem to be exploding outside. Yet the sea isn't even visible; all he can see is a luminous sunset sky over sandhills stretching both ways as far as the eye can reach.

The memory of a hot uncomfortable drive from the port comes back to him as though he'd dreamt it, together with his premonition that Luz won't be here; which the neglected, abandoned aspect of the hotel at once confirms... while at the same time it seems to remind him of something in his own past.... But the place must be occupied, after all, for before he can recall the association, he's confronted by a youth whose nude torso matches the batik pattern of his skirt, which in turn merges with the shadows beginning to coagulate in the room, so that his figure is altogether somewhat indefinite, even ghostly. Disconcerted by his sudden, silent, unexpected arrival, Luke wonders where on earth he has sprung from... then, assuming he's one of the houseboys, asks whether a fair-haired girl is staying there, and if so, which is her cabin. He has to repeat the question, and still isn't sure it has been understood, as the other only makes a vague gesture, and immediately afterwards vanishes as suddenly as he came.

Again Luke is considerably taken aback. And, as he's already a bit confused, he gets the impression he must have imagined the incident... or else that he's just seen an apparition. He has no intention of investigating any of the cabins; so his bewilderment increases when he finds himself climbing the steps of one.... All this seems to be happening to him in a dream.... However, since he's here, he decides that he may as well look inside, and peers into the bedroom; which is too dark for him to make out anything clearly. Something white hanging on the wall might be a coat or a dressing-gown; there's no reason, anyhow, to connect it with Luz. And the other white blur of the mosquito-net over the bed is as impersonal as a small diaphanous cloud.

At least he has established the fact that Luz herself is not in the hotel. Suddenly, thinking this, he feels he has done all that can be expected, needn't bother about her any further, and hurries outside again. Instantly his eyes and thoughts turn to the distant mountains, which are the home of the legendary singing lemurs he loves so much – his feeling for them is almost metaphysical. More than anything in the world, he wants to devote himself to them, and now he must surely be free to do so, as he hasn't found the girl. But the point seems doubtful. The mountains themselves have withdrawn from sight into the approaching darkness. Although sunset rose still lingers over the sea, the sky inland has already retired into night. Besides, he feels none of the euphoria, the sensation of confident rightness he experienced when he first decided to dedicate his life to the study of the strange singers.

Disappointed, he slowly descends the steps to the darkening garden, the dunes looming ahead like a fortified wall between dark and day. But his mood swings upward when he notices the car he came in still standing at the door of the main building. On the spot he's convinced that it's waiting for him ... the driver must know by telepathy that he means to leave ... or why is he still there? Everything's going to work out right for him after all. He has only to get back into the car and be driven away from this place for ever. As he hurries along, eager to get going, his feet seem to avoid by instinct the various plants and obstacles it's already too dark to see.

He keeps looking at the car, expecting the driver to emerge and speak to him. But he doesn't ... there's not a sound ... no movement is visible in the dim interior of the vehicle, although he fancies he can distinguish a huddled figure behind the wheel. Thinking the fellow must have dropped off to sleep, he's about to shout to him when he steps on a fallen branch which saves him the trouble, snapping under his weight with a noise like a rifle-shot, loud enough to rouse anyone.

Still nothing happens. Nobody stirs in the car, even now. And at last he's forced to realize that it's empty; he has just imagined the figure inside. Of course the driver had plenty of time to walk off while he was seeing his 'apparition'. And while there was still enough light, it never occurred to him to look and see if a real person was sitting in the big car.

*

Apparition? Telepathy? With faint astonishment, Luke found the two words circulating in his head, unrelated, apparently, to any particular happening. He would have to wait for this confused feeling to wear off... this vagueness... before deciding what to do next. In the meanwhile he walked on mechanically and crossed the garden without noticing it, hardly conscious of his feet sinking into the coarser, looser sand of the dunes, still warm from the sun.

His head was aching, but this didn't worry him specially. A sort of woolliness obscured his thoughts, but in no way interfered with his climbing up and down sandy slopes. No grass, no vegetation of any kind, grew here, so he didn't have to bother about invisible obstacles, which was fortunate, as he couldn't see where he was putting his feet. The sunset had faded out almost entirely, reduced to one pallid streak in the process of being obliterated by blue-black darkness spreading over his head. Behind him big stars were coming out one by one, disseminating a faint glaze, which resembled, but wasn't exactly, light – the moon would soon provide that, a paler patch of sky already indicated where it would rise.

So far he hadn't caught sight of the sea, and its sound was still muffled; he must be walking parallel to it, he supposed vaguely. It was easy walking here, even pleasant, in spite of deep cuttings between the dunes made by flood-water or the encroaching tide – avoiding these without difficulty, he kept on at an easy pace, as if walking on soft warm cushions. The moist tropical air was slowly cooling off now that the sun had gone. Nevertheless, the effort of walking was making him sweat, though he was unaware of this, only dimly reflecting how smoothly everything seemed to be going.

Too smoothly.... An ominous sense of fatality abruptly insinuated inself among his confused ideas, as if fate were conducting him to an unavoidable, unknown, but certainly unpleasant conclusion.

He suddenly felt helpless and almost frightened, like someone who begins to suspect he is the victim of a huge, cruel, grotesque practical joke. His alarm increased, as, in a barely describable flash of insight, he saw himself involved in something immense, insensate, incomprehensible, that was happening all round him... involved in it up to the hilt, without the remotest chance of escape... utterly at the mercy of this nameless thing, for which even the concept of mercy was non-existent....

The sound of the breakers suddenly loud in his ears, he pulled himself up abruptly and just in time, the ball of his foot crumbling sand on the edge of nothing. At the same moment, the moon sprang into the sky, flooding everything with white light, revealing how precariously he was balanced on the crest of one of the highest dunes, just where its sandy lip crumbled into a sheer drop, the ocean outspread before him. Hastily stepping back to a safer position, he had the momentary illusion that there were *two* moons... that he was seeing double... until he realized that one was the reflection, floating and flickering in the shallows, of the one sailing majestically up the sky.

*

With his first glance, he has already recognized the nude girlish figure, slight as a child's, in the hollow below him... remembering rather than seeing the dark terrified glitter of the dilated eyes in the paper-white face she lifts towards him. The moon grows more brilliant each second, and seems to focus on her like a stage spotlight, painting unnatural black pits of shadow in the hollows of her white flesh. Her white albino hair sparkles like running water, shimmering round her head in a dazzling sheen of light and feathery spray. His mind blank, he stares down at her as if mesmerized, from that high edge of sand, between the moon and the sea.

Suddenly she spins round, white dazzle still ringing her head, and takes a few stiff, unsteady, running steps away from him like a clockwork toy... the mechanism of which abruptly breaks or runs down... perhaps she trips over some piece of detritus, or catches her foot in loose sand... begins, anyhow, for whatever reason, to stagger and stumble and start falling....

With no recollection of slithering down the steep slope, he finds himself close beside her, where she's half kneeling, half crouching, on the white sand, her head bent and her face hidden. The moon has become still more brilliant, unpleasantly, almost unbearably, bright. He notices this even though his attention is concentrated on the small firm globes of her breasts, tipped with pagoda-shaped nipples. The flood of light falls like white fire from the sky on her glittering hair, the ruffled surface of which is stirring continuously in minute complex convolutions – he seems to feel them weaving crazily in his head, and looks away, dazzled.

But there's the same brutally bright moonlight wherever he looks, the same relentless white blaze pours down upon everything. The whole beach is a glaring white dazzle, each small wave as it breaks leaves behind a semicircle of glistening foam; and all these white intersecting curves combine with the bright sand in a twofold brilliance, like a long stretch of dazzling snow, where the occasional sharp edge of a broken shell glitters icily.

With an impatient movement, he again changes the direction of his gaze. But still the moonlight is inescapable. He's disgusted to see it glinting on the buttons of his jacket: simultaneously feeling the flare of white light pounding down on his head and shoulders. The weight of the entire sky seems to press on the top of his head, which now aches as if about to split open. He can't stand the pressure... it's insufferable.... He clenches his fists, struggling desperately against the hateful thrill of excitement it generates in him, listening at the same time to his own rapid breathing... or is it the little waves he hears lapping the sand with a sound like hurried, excited gasps?

His eyes are drawn back irresistibly to the trembling victim, whose slender limbs slash across his eyeballs in brilliant flashes. Her hair falls around her in sparkling showers, sending out blinding flashes like electricity.

A long thin glittering blade of delirious joy pierces his head... his hand imperceptibly starts moving towards her. His eyes never leave the back of her frail neck, where there's a pathetic little hollow between two prominent sinews, a tender, vulnerable spot, into which a knife would sink without any resistance... which deepens, intoxicatingly exposed, as her head bends lower. Emitting sparks of white fire, her hair glides over her shoulders in two dazzling cascades... deep into his brain....

Something blindingly bright strikes his forehead, as, with set teeth, he seizes her arm, which jerks feebly and frantically in his grasp. Just for an instant he's aware of the blows of the moon thudding silently on his head and shoulders... then only of the insupportable complexity of the excitement surging within him... while he grips her other arm, dragging her up and towards him....

Terror, like an electric shock, galvanizes her into violent struggles, gives her demented strength. And he, unprepared for such sudden intense opposition, has to let her go. A whole flight of fiery blades pierces his head like a burst of meteors, splitting it wide open, so that he clutches it with both hands, trying to hold it together... forgetting everything else temporarily... feeling as though his brains were trickling away into the soft dry sand.... His thoughts are in utter chaos... he's a whirlpool of inexpressible emotions....

When after a timeless confused interval he slowly comes back to himself, his excitement has left him completely – it's as if it had never been. He doesn't even see his companion at first, blinded by the sweat or tears running down his cheeks.

She is standing only a few inches away from him, her face deathly white in the glare of the moon, panting from the tremendous physical effort of freeing herself, her whole slight body shaken, as it would be by violent sobs, by her quick, painful breathing. Probably she is incapable of further movement. And as he doesn't move either, they keep these relative positions, separated by a small gap, staring into each other's moon-blanched faces.

Until, suddenly, at exactly the same moment, with the same strange, despairing, spontaneous impulse, they move closer, and, without embracing or speaking, simply stand clinging together, like two terrified children.

 A PETER OWEN PAPERBACK